THE MODEL

D1730591

The Model

ROBERT AICKMAN

FABER & FABER

This edition first published in 2014
by Faber and Faber Ltd
Bloomsbury House, 74–77 Great Russell Street
London WC1B 3DA

Printed and bound by CPI Group (UK) Ltd, Croydon, CRO 4YY

A CIP record for this book is available from the British Library

ISBN 978-0-571-31682-3

THE MODEL

All history is fiction, just as all fiction is history
—Benedetto Croce

Elena sprawled on the hard chair with her legs as far apart as her skirt would stretch. She had abandoned even that simplest of tasks, the pulling the stalks off cherries which were about to be plunged into the strongest of spirit in order to sustain the family and their friends through the winter, now only a week or two ahead at the best. Elena gazed almost perpendicularly at the freckled ceiling. There were times when she positively wished she were a boy, though not a boy like her brothers, Gregori and Boris.

Gregori and Boris, with hardly a year between them, were enormously older than Elena: as good as grown up ever since she had known them, or as bad. Her dear friend Mikhail, the son of the priest, though only a little younger than Boris, was not grown up: he wrote epic poems, he painted mysterious pictures, as small as the poems were large, he played the balalaika, and, when out of earshot, he sang. He sang holy songs, of course, but sometimes, when out with Elena in the woods and meadows, songs that were more personal, and personal to her, as Elena knew quite well. She found it hard to imagine Mikhail being grown up ever, even though various horrid transformations in trusted people had already come her way.

Boris, the younger of her brothers, was so much older

than she was that she wondered how she had come to be born at all, and many others wondered also, including some who had been intimately concerned in the matter. Since Gregori and Boris, there had been many miscarriages, and several sad stillbirths.

Elena's best friend, Tatiana Ivanovna, suggested that Elena might be a changeling: the offspring of gypsies, or of the nobility, or of fairies, or of spirits.

"*Happy* spirits," said Tatiana, who was always cheerful and kind.

"I don't think I *look* like a *gypsy,*" said Elena gravely, who was blond almost to whiteness. But the other possibilities remained, and there were many more also. Children who were uncertain of their parentage abounded. Elena knew that it was the kind of thing to be expected. No one had told her so. She knew.

One might have supposed that as the youngest and coming so late, Elena would have been fussed and pampered, perhaps to spoliation. Such was not the case. Her mother was worn out and dispirited, virtually an invalid. Her father, the best lawyer in the small town, was much preoccupied with trying to collect his fees, in order that the family could survive. With almost all his clients almost always in default, he was in a position to allow himself few pleasures, or his family either. He had once been a great sportsman. In that way he had won patronage, and had added to the number and importance of his clients, backsliders though they were.

By now Gregori was in the army and doing very well at a great distance; and Boris was in a seminary, reporting very little. All the priests Elena had met, including Mikhail's father, had been stalwart, muscular men, visibly akin to Boris; as ready to tackle a miscreant in the material world as to combat the demons of sloth and pride in the spiritual.

In the empty house Elena might for long periods have been totally forgotten and even unfed had it not been for Bábaba. Bábaba was nursemaid and nanny, governess and preceptor, mother and grandmother and guardian angel; and so many other things also that Elena had lost count. It was Bábaba who had set Elena now to stalking the cherries.

One difficult matter was that, contrary to first appearances, the stalks simply would not come away without drawing half the cherry with them, so that the basic task soon seemed to Elena pointless. Elena was one who reached decisions of that kind quite rapidly (only, of course, when the circumstances justified). In the present case, however, as so often in life, there was a simple and factual explanation: the cherries set aside for submerging in strong spirit were those deemed too tough, hard, and generally inferior for presentation at the Timorasiev table.

It was Cook who had separated the goats from the sheep; Cook who had no other name than Cook, and never had had, or could have had. Cook had hurled the bullety fruit at Bábaba, indicating that she would want it back by that evening for the distillation or the predistillation, or for some vital preliminary even to that. Cook's hands were too full for the stalking of fruit, and the kitchen girl, Asmara, was coughing so badly these days as to be unable to work at all. Asmara squatted all the time in the corner, simply coughing and retching. She would probably have been provided with consolatory texts if she had been able to read. Elena, who was sorry for her, sometimes secreted her a bonbon, emanating ultimately from the priest's sister, Tosha, who made bonbons all day, summer and winter, selling them where she could, giving them away where she felt fond, melting them down again where she had to.

Cook's hands would, therefore, have been sufficiently full in any case, but as things were, work had been unceasing for days because guests were expected, and foreign guests, though old friends.

Elena never forgot that it was precisely at that moment, without meaning, when her eyes were looking upwards and seeing nothing, and the bucket of mangled cherries was between her open legs, that Herr and Frau Barger von Meyrendorff entered the house through the door used by tradesmen, children, and hens. They had arrived a whole day and three-quarters early, owing to the new railroad, in every way superlative! Papa had either overlooked its existence or gravely miscalculated its functioning. In order to keep down the number of problems and demands, the Timorasiev family made no use of the railroad themselves.

"Ma petite!" cried Frau Barger von Meyrendorff, and threw her arms tightly round Elena, lifting her feet many inches from the floor. *"Chérie!"* she gasped, covering Elena with kisses all over her face and childishly bare neck.

"We failed to obtain entry through the front door," said Herr Barger von Meyrendorff, beaming.

"But we regard you, Elena, as nearly the head of the family now," said Frau von Meyrendorff jocularly, at last setting her more or less upon her feet; "with your brothers all those thousands of leagues distant, and possibly never to return, or not for a very long time."

"We have brought gifts to the little Elena," cried Herr von Meyrendorff, radiant with sentiment. "She is an important person now."

He was holding out a colored object, which previously he had been concealing behind his frock coat.

"Merci beaucoup," said Elena politely, though still gasping slightly. "What is it?" She hesitated to lay hands upon it without first finding out, though Tatiana, her friend, would have seized it at once, with no questions asked.

"You have three chances to find out," cried Herr von Meyrendorff, superfluously elevating the object beyond Elena's immediate reach.

"It's a fairy lantern," said Elena, less gravely than when she spoke to Tatiana or even to Mikhail; more in the carefree manner that grown-up people liked and used among themselves, when not in tears or in a rage.

"No."

"It's a funny game to play."

"No. Wrong again. It's not a game at all." Herr von Meyrendorff was almost bursting with suffocated mirth.

"It's a fruit. Like a popomack."

"Very nearly right, little lady. But it's not a popomack. It's an *ananas.*"

Elena had never seen a pineapple, or even a picture of one, nor even heard of such a thing's existence.

"What's that?" she inquired doubtfully.

"It's a very big, very choice fruit, *chérie,*" explained Frau von Meyrendorff, tenderly. "You slice it up with a silver knife, and you eat all of it, every bit of it, and it will bring you luck."

Of course, grown-ups always used those last words when they were wanting to be nice and to make the impression they intended; and so far the words had meant nothing very much.

"Yes, *you* eat *all* of it," said Herr von Meyrendorff with enormous double emphasis, and perhaps double meaning too. "You don't give away any of it to anyone."

"Except tiny bits to us," put in Frau von Meyrendorff merrily.

"But secretly," said Herr von Meyrendorff with the same gigantic emphasis. "You must keep the whole thing secret, or bits of *ananas* will find their way into the wrong hands."

"I shall give bits to Tatiana and Ismene and Clémence and Mikhail," said Elena.

"Yes, to *them*," said Frau von Meyrendorff, defining by omission.

"I won't cry catch, as it's rather spiny and spiky," said Herr von Meyrendorff. "If you'll hold out both your hands, I'll put it in them."

Doubtfully, Elena did as she had been told.

"Ouch," she cried. "It's like a porcupine."

"How often have your hands held a porcupine?" inquired Frau von Meyrendorff.

"Only once," replied Elena truthfully. "But for two whole minutes. Then it jumped down and ran away."

"*Dommage,*" said Frau von Meyrendorff. "But never mind. I have a present for you too. Put down the porcupine, and accept a present from me. My present is wrapped in silver paper, and tied with scarlet ribbon, and you are to promise not to open it until you are in your little bedroom, and entirely alone."

In point of fact, Elena's bedroom was far from being little, and immediately above it was a whole floor of empty attics; many of them. Elena was far from sure how many there were. On the other hand she was perfectly sure about being alone in her bedroom. She was almost always alone there. Not even Bábaba had ever once been permitted to sleep with her. Elena's mother was obsessed with the need for hygiene, and always had been.

Once more, Elena silently stretched out her white hands.

"You have the hands and wrists of an artist, my little child," said Herr von Meyrendorff, rather seriously.

Elena stared at her hands, dazed and spellbound for a second, but confused. Mikhail had tried to teach her to paint and draw, to write poetry, and to sing, all with little success, and had sadly concluded that she would never be an artist at all. He had told her so in the nicest way, and wept.

"Don't forget, you must promise," said Frau von Meyrendorff gently.

Elena looked up. "I promise," she said, without much thought.

And then Frau von Meyrendorff's present was in her arms. Somehow, somewhere, it had been successfully concealed until that moment. It was less heavy than she expected, but the silver paper gleamed and glinted in the fading light, the glow of autumn, as everyone everywhere called it, and all the time.

"Elena Andreievna Timorasieva!" cried out a clear voice from the deeper gloom within the house. *"Donnez-moi cet objet là, immédiatement!"*

But, by the mercy of the Holy Ones, it was at the hideous, hairy pineapple that Bábaba was so relentlessly pointing, not at the silvery mystery, held tight to Elena's bosom.

"That is no food for a child," proclaimed Bábaba, the compassionate.

"It is the most healthy food a child could eat, or a grown-up person either," said Herr Barger von Meyrendorff, his cheeks mantling as far as one could see through the dusk. "Life is far too short for abstinence of any kind."

"I am not speaking of grown-up persons," said Bábaba. "The little ones have to be protected and defended against novelties and impurities of all kinds, and specially little girls." Bábaba was courageously clutching the pineapple to her chest, spines and all, exactly as Elena was holding the silvery mystery.

"Impurities! How dare you employ such a word?" rejoined Herr von Meyrendorff, now, almost certainly, more black in the face than red. "Have I not seven daughters of my own, six grown to maidenhood?"

"Yes, it is so," confirmed Frau von Meyrendorff.

"Madame decides what is to be eaten in this house, what is to be done, what is to be thought and felt. I am only a servant, but I am closer to Madame than a shadow, and closer than a shadow to Elena Andreievna too."

"Return me that fruit at once!" demanded Herr von Meyrendorff, advancing upon Bábaba, through the gloaming, presumably in order to take possession.

"Amadeus, be controlled," recommended Frau von Meyrendorff.

But the apparition of Herr von Meyrendorff was already so alarming that Bábaba temporized, mighty fortress though she was.

"I shall take the object to Madame, when Madame has finished resting. Hers will be the final word upon the subject."

"No," said Herr von Meyrendorff. "Return the fruit to me at this moment, and, if I and my wife think fit, it is we who shall address Madame Timorasieva in our own persons."

But by then Elena had crept away in the darkness. Clinging to the silvery package, she climbed flight after flight of stairs, cast open the door of her huge bedroom, carefully shut the door behind her as Frau von Meyrendorff had directed, and threw herself on the big bed. There had never been any intermediate condition for Elena between cramped cot and this dimly painted bed that would have held twelve Elenas, three at the head, and three at the foot, and three on each side, as in the picture.

Elena slowly and carefully untied the silk ribbon and dismantled the silver paper, the finest and the most she had ever seen. Within was another wrapping paper, dark in the darkness. There was no knowing what hue it was. And at the heart of it all was simply a book.

Elena had expected something entirely new and unknown, either fanciful or instructive, for she was often a serious little girl. She was exceedingly disappointed. She feared that the book might even be in German, of which she thought she knew but a single word, which she had lately learned and which was *Kirschwasser*. But no: at least the book seemed to be in French. Mamma had always insisted that all possible domestic and social communication be in French and upon all visitors speaking in French, wherever they might have come from. By the very last of the daylight Elena could just make out the book's title: it was *Les coryphées de la petite cave.* Elena was but little the wiser.

She laid the book on the bedside chest of drawers and applied herself to folding the silver paper into the neatest possible package, and then the other paper also. In almost total darkness she deposited the paper and the book in a useful cavity she had found and enlarged in the wall paneling behind the icon. It was not a completely secret hiding place but, to reach it, a grown-up person would probably have to move the icon, which would have been sacrilegious.

In the end Bábaba would be coming after her with a lamp, but Elena knew that in the meanwhile Bábaba would attend upon Madame, to whom her first duty lay, and the duration of whose needs and commands was unpredictable, even when she was asleep. The tiny flame before the icon was insufficient even for reading French, and there was nothing for Elena to do but straighten her hair and her dress and to think. She was already a practiced thinker. She sometimes decided that she thought more than all the rest of the household put together. She passed the fine foreign ribbon through her fingers again and again, and round and back, taking care, however, not to crease, crumple, or spoil it. A length of fine scarlet ribbon might in the end come in useful for almost anything.

It was not Bábaba who appeared, but Frau von Meyrendorff. She came steaming in like a locomotive which

had ascended a long and notorious incline. She was carrying
a lamp, though guests seldom succeeded in taking lamps
from the rooms without authority. The lamplight beautifully illumined Frau von Meyrendorff's red-and-gold hair,
large brown eyes, large but soft-looking nose, and large
mouth.

The first thing she did was set the lamp on the bedside
chest of drawers where, had she but known, her present had
lately lain, and the next thing was once more to gather up
Elena into her arms, so that Elena would again have to
straighten her hair and dress, those things at least.

"My little love!" gurgled Frau von Meyrendorff. "My
darling! My perfect, silky doll!"

Elena recollected that all but one of Frau von Meyrendorff's own daughters were now grown up, and therefore
likely to be found at arm's length.

"Thank you for the book, Frau von Meyrendorff,"
said Elena, as soon as she was able to speak at all.

"Where is the book?" asked Frau von Meyrendorff,
looking eagerly round the room, but not again picking up the
lamp, which was hissing slightly and smelling so that one
noticed.

"I have put it away," said Elena judiciously. "It lies
with my treasures."

"You are quite right to do so, Elena," said Frau von
Meyrendorff, but still looking about her, as if the book might
stalk on legs from the wainscot, as in the familiar tale. "The

theme is somewhat complex for a young girl, but I take the view that you will not be a young girl always, and Amadeus, my husband, agreed when I said that."

"Indeed, no," said Elena. "I expect to be married and to have at least as many children as you, Frau von Meyrendorff."

"I am not sure the book will help in that direction," said Frau von Meyrendorff, chuckling lightly.

"Bábaba says that *everything* helps in that direction, and that things should be shunned that do not."

Elena was combing her hair, once more so tangled.

"Bábaba is herself an unmarried woman, Elena. It is necessary for me to point that out."

"But she is so wise and kind, Frau von Meyrendorff. I depend upon her entirely, and Mamma does also. Bábaba knows all that it is needful for me to know. She always tells me that, and Mamma tells me so too."

"Your Mother and I were at school together, you know, Elena. It was in Paris, the capital of France."

"Yes, I know, Frau von Meyrendorff, though Mamma does not speak of it."

"There were English girls and Spanish girls, as well as French, German, and Russian girls. There was even a girl from India. She counted as English, of course. How we all loved her!"

"I love Mikhail, Frau von Meyrendorff, though he's much, much older than I am."

"A very good choice, I'm sure, Elena, and one that I am certain you have kept to yourself until this moment."

"Yes," said Elena, quite simply.

"Let me help you with that comb, my child. Your hair is so very pale and abundant. It is like flax."

Elena sank her face into Frau von Meyrendorff's tight white blouse, while that lady combed away in short strokes over the top of Elena's head.

"Mikhail says my hair is like the hair of an angel in an Italian picture," muttered Elena, hardly able to make the words audible.

"That is true, Elena," replied Frau von Meyrendorff, disentangling ever more vigorously. "Though we must never forget modesty. I wonder if that lamp contains the right kerosene? In one's own home and homeland one can feel assured of such things. Elsewhere one cannot. If it will light us down all those flights of stairs, you may watch me change my clothes for the repast ahead of us."

"I shall not be at the repast, Frau von Meyrendorff. Bábaba will bring me *korchina* up here."

"And later," promised Frau von Meyrendorff, "I shall reascend the Jungfrau and bring you some delicacies from the table."

Elena curtsied. In the lamplight the curtsy looked almost dashing.

"Come, child," cried Frau von Meyrendorff, lifting her skirt in her free hand, "come away now. Time is short."

But Frau von Meyrendorff did not reappear that night, though Elena remained sleepless for hours.

She was perfectly accustomed to grown-ups behaving like that, but was disappointed all the same, by Frau von Meyrendorff, whom she had last seen in the loveliest pink dress, sprinkled with scores of even pinker camellias, all handmade.

Still, in the end, the first faint light of dawn crept in, and the heavy autumn rain seeped in, harbinger of snow, endless snow, of floods, of agues, of a new year. Elena stole from her dimly painted bed and tiptoed across the room, even though, to the best of her belief, there was no one near her, either to the left or to the right, below her, or (most certainly not) above her. Her nightdress had been made for her by Tatiana, who had given it her on her day. Later Bábaba had made a great fuss about the colored strips and stripes that adorned it, and had never since ceased alluding to them. Elena took her new book from its little grotto behind the icon and flitted back to the warm blankets. From the bed the tiny light of devotion was always invisible for a certain period of the dawn.

The book described a group of young girls who dwelt together in what was virtually a cellar, near the Cimetière du Nord, and worked together in the ballet of the opera, though in the lowest grade. To a few came promotion into a higher grade and departure from the cellar. Certain girls, upon promotion failing to come, or true love either, hurled or lowered themselves into the Seine, beautiful though they were. Most found neither promotion nor release, but rather dressmaking jobs, little shops, husbands, elderly relatives to care for and tend, lives very like the lives of others who had never received their long training or suffered their deep dedication. The last chapters of the book considered these ultimate destinies of the girls, lined up as if for a roll call.

"Holy Seraphina!" thought Elena, as she read. "How necessary it is to be young!" She reflected for a moment, then added to herself, "Even with Mikhail!"

Two of the girls in the book died of wasting disease, one in a grim sanatorium. Many of them bore children, within wedlock or without, but the children were considered mainly in their financial or economic aspect, as was so much else. There were unnumbered affairs of the heart, a few true and tender, and, of course, close friendships sometimes between the girls themselves. One of the girls, one only, had become a ballerina, but by then none of the others seemed to envy her. Not once did any girl say she did.

Elena, however, envied her very much.

There was a whole short chapter given to a detailed account of her day, and of her night. The other dancers standing aside as she entered the practice room and, later, falling back in awe as she practiced; the manager of the opera pampering and humoring her; the storms of applause when she swept onto the stage, the greater storms when she swept off it, the tornado at her curtain calls; the night of champagne (French champagne), slavery, and passion, all in the company of a

Grand Duke, actually a real Grand Duke, who seemed, in the main, a larger and, naturally, grander version of Mikhail himself, poetry, singing, love, and all the rest. Taller, larger, more muscular, and very, very much richer, but basically the same.

The Grand Duke, visiting Paris on undefined state business, fell in love for life with the ballerina when first he beheld her at the center of the vast stage in a ballet named "La Belle Ensorceleuse," incident to an opera of some kind. Unfortunately, the book did not make clear whether there really was such an opera, as seemed very likely, or whether it had been invented but not composed by the guileful author. Who was the author? Elena turned back to look. He was himself a member of the nobility: Baron de la Touque; though there was provided no likeness of him. At the time the Grand Duke fell in love with her for life the ballerina had had a lover already, a French Marquis, named Raoul, but the Grand Duke slew him the very next day in a duel, indeed at dawn, much the hour at which Elena was reading about it. Heavy autumn rainfall was not mentioned as an accompaniment of the duel.

Elena, who, as has been stated, had had much time for thinking, understood quite clearly that the author's intention was to contrast the glittering fruits of fame with the quieter rewards of ordinary, normal life.

Frau von Meyrendorff had indicated that the lessons of the book were of an advanced and difficult kind for one who was still a young girl. Perhaps, moreover, Frau von Meyrendorff had not herself read every word of the book, as often proved to be the case with grown-ups and the books they gave away.

It was amazing how wide a knowledge of life in every single aspect was displayed by the noble author! Elena felt that his understanding of the female soul in all its varied possibilities was particularly extraordinary. Mamma had always said there were no people like French people. Here was an example of it: the first, as it happened, that Elena had actually encountered for herself, instead of merely being told about, often rather boringly. On the other hand, the Frenchman in the book had been instantly shot dead by a Russian. That had to be borne in mind also. And doubtless it would have been the same with *épées,* had the *épées* been removed from their cases.

Bábaba always said that if Elena did not wish to appear for her morning guinea fowl egg, then she needn't. She, Bábaba, had enough to do without looking after people who could very well look after themselves but wouldn't be bothered.

That morning, Elena did not wish.

Not even when she had finished the book, and then reread the first chapter of it. There was further thinking to be done first.

The first chapter described the training needed before a girl could even hope to dance in ballet at the opera. In the rest of the book Elena had noted for herself that, though some of the girls killed themselves from disappointment, none seemed even to think of applying to dance elsewhere. She had also noted that the occasional men, men rather than boys, the "partners," seemed to dance without training. They certainly did not train with the girls, who lived like novices, or were supposed to; and there was no reference to their training anywhere else: their partnership seemed simply to be a fact of life, as so often with men. Men were given to one, already perfect, or as accomplished as could be expected. Not one of the girls married her partner, in any case. If they married at all, they married clerks, soldiers, or kind and gentle watchmakers in later middle age. Ballerinas married devoted men who helped with their careers. Grand Dukes were not for marrying because they already had wives at home in Russia. With them romance had to suffice. But whatever else matters, speculated Elena; at least to a female? She could think of nothing.

Elena could not indite poems, could not limn flowers or peasants, could not strum or warble, but yet she was an artist. Herr Amadeus Barger von Meyrendorff had said so very specifically, only yesterday. Elena, as it happened, had needed no telling, but she had been grateful for the confirmation; so grateful that she had instantly fainted away, though only for a split second. Herr von Meyrendorff had cited her wrists and hands. What could he know of her ankles and feet?

Aflame, despite the weather, with conviction, Elena sped down for her guinea fowl egg, after all; and kind Bábaba, conspicuously padded and coiffed, cooked it for her, commenting continuously. It was always Bábaba, and not Cook, who prepared Elena's egg. Cook at that hour (as at most hours) had other, far more important things to do.

"And why are you not wearing your warm tunic and skirt, Elena Andreievna?"

"I forgot, Bábaba."

"Have you not felt the cold rain?"

"Not yet, Bábaba."

"The stove does not suffice for your Mother, Elisavetta Pavlovna. She has also called for two kerosene heaters as well. Soon she will demand more."

"I hope it's the right kerosene."

"That is the concern of Stefan Triforovitch. It is he who works in the woodhouse, the oilhouse, the coalhouse. I cannot do everything outside and inside, especially now that winter is here."

"It is not winter yet, Bábaba."

"The guinea fowl have already stopped laying, Elena Andreievna. That means it is winter."

"Where is Frau von Meyrendorff?"

Elena really asked because the whole house had seemed so quiet as she descended, and seemed so quiet now. There was only Stefan chopping, against the winter; and Cook macerating old walnuts, grunting whenever she macerated a thumb also.

"Herr and Frau von Meyrendorff have left us."

"But they were to have stayed three weeks!"

"Their plans have changed."

"But why, Bábaba?"

"How should I know?"

Elena was certain that Bábaba did know, if only because Bábaba knew everything that was needful.

"Was there a quarrel, Bábaba?"

"Eat your radishes, Elena Andreievna."

"Is Mamma prostrate?"

"Your poor Mother is in the arms of Our Redeemer, Elena Andreievna. As always."

Bábaba crossed herself not once but twice. Elena knew it to be an obscure quittance for whatever had happened.

Elena stole upstairs, not to her bedroom, but higher still. Elena did not consider that it was particularly cold. She suspected, indeed, that the rain implied a certain extra warmth or mugginess, perhaps not very wholesome. She looked for a moment through one of the dirty windows. From this altitude she could distinctly see the marshes steaming. Her father owed it to his position to occupy one of the tallest houses in the small town, combining dignity with the possibility of wide circumspection.

Elena set herself to making a model.

Gregori and Boris had left up here their many boxes of tools, over which they had fought one another so regularly and bitterly. Distant relative after distant relative, accepted family friend after accepted family friend, elderly foreign visitor after elderly foreign visitor, all had given the boys boxes of tools; far too often with the smiling hope that the two of them would share the gift. Even when a gift was bestowed upon one lad individually, the other preferred the component parts of it to those of his own. Elena's Mother had always needed foreign visitors, even elderly visitors. Whenever she had the strength, she wrote long letters to far places, mostly in France; illegible letters, because written in bed. The tools brought from the other side of the European land mass amazed everybody, but inevitably led to worse than ever fraternal strife, to dust stirred up and shaken down everywhere in the house, and in the attic turmoil inconceivable.

When the boys were out all day shooting and trapping, Elena had managed to teach herself more about the use of tools than would be found in any rulebook. Of course Silke had helped greatly, even though a cripple and almost unbelievably slow of speech. Silke was supposed to be a direct descendant of a Prussian who had invaded the country with Napoleon and somehow been left behind. Silke couldn't do much for himself but there was no limit to what he would do for Elena.

"*You* ought to have been a great strong boy, Elena Andreievna," Silke would say, taking half a minute to complete the sentence.

"No, thank you, Silke," Elena would regularly, and more readily, reply.

Now, in the course of half one single rainy morning and part of an afternoon, Elena, using saws, hammers, nails, and dubious glue, completed the outer framework of an entire opera house, and also installed nearly half the stage.

Meals were irregular in the Timorasiev house, perhaps because the master simply lacked time for them. Vodka and cold cabbage alone sustained him as the proceedings he was always having to take against his different clients came to court or to some less formal assize.

The opera house was complete in less than four days, even though a Sunday had intervened. Nor was Elena's more prosaic education delayed or impaired: which took place on several afternoons a week, in company with Tatiana, Ismene, and Clémence, under the direction of a pretty governess, Mademoiselle Olivier-Page. The lessons were at the villa of Tatiana's Mamma, a widow. It was less than a verst away, and Tatiana's Mamma gave all the little girls tea and rich cakes every time they were there. Clémence was Mademoiselle Olivier-Page's niece, the brightest of the class at book learning. All the girls loved their lessons and were eager for more, provided the lessons would not interfere with the serious purposes of life, such as that upon which Elena was now embarked. Happily, they seldom did.

Not only the illustrations in her new book (or some of them) told Elena what a place of public entertainment looked like. There was a theater in the town itself, built when a bygone Tsar or Tsarina was supposed to be paying the place a visit. Possibly it had been used then; certainly it had never been used since. One reason was that the town itself was plainly too small to provide an audience for so huge an establishment, and there was no other community of size nearer than Smorevsk, seventy-two versts distant. The enlistment in sufficient number of actors, actresses, singers, dancers, and musicians would have been another difficult matter. Mikhail could have essayed most of these professions, but there were simply not enough like him. The theater was used mainly for the storage of casks of vodka and of a reed beer brewed exclusively in the locality. Tatiana used to make eyes at the porters, who were all aged and sodden, so that she and Elena knew by now every corner of the place. Often Ismene came too, who mainly liked hanging from the flies, as from a trapeze, and waving herself about: something she could not do at home, nor would have been permitted to do. Ismene's father was the head both of the police and of the secret police, and Ismene was an only child. The girls used even to run the big curtain up and down, straining, all three of them, on the winch, and filling the place with dust, though the old porters coughed so much anyway that the extra dust made little difference. That, of course, was if they were not asleep at the time, and loudly snoring. When the curtain was more or less up, and the winch chocked, the girls used to take it in turns to stand stage center and drop most graceful curtsies, nor did they dispute as to who should curtsy first or last.

Elena could hardly be unaware, therefore, of the need for a curtain in her own opera house. She gazed at her green velvet cloak, scissors in hand (one of the toolboxes had actually contained these scissors, which were almost as long as Elena's shin); her green cloak, lined with pure, pink satin, as it hung in its cupboard. She then stole down three flights of stairs to her Mother's bedroom. She tapped.

"Mamma!"

She tapped again.

"Mamma! Mamma!"

The note of anguish was necessary if the test of Mamma's current wakefulness was to be dependable.

Elena softly opened the door and more softly still opened the huge wardrobe filled with outdoor things no longer used. The room contained a third kerosene heater, and eight somber icons, and a clockwork machine that clicked and threw different colors on the mottled ceiling. Mamma was simply shapeless, scarcely stirring.

Upstairs once more, Elena mopped her brow and neck and applied herself to her own small scissors, curvaceous and silvery, and her needle. She was less adroit with these implements than with certain others, but within twenty-five minutes the curtain was ready for hanging and trimming.

The color, a deepish blue, appealed less to Elena than the green of her own cloak, and the paler blue lining was positively obvious, but the signs of wear upon the velvet made the opera house look long established instead of merely childish and imitative, and of that Elena could only approve. In any case, her book had spoken of blue hangings garnishing a ballet named "The Queen of the Night," part of an opera by Mozart, though Elena would have liked a colored illustration to indicate the exact hue. Imperfection, always imperfection: there was not a single colored illustration in the book, not even of the Café des Hirondelles.

That same evening, as dusk was slowly falling yet again, Elena provided the bottom of the curtain with a wide silvery fringe, which originated in a headdress she had worn as a Girl from Tashkent at one of Tatiana's Mother's tea parties.

She would have to devise a machine for raising and lowering the two parts of the curtain, and also to paint the entire structure, outside austerely, inside sparklingly. The interior of every box would be in a different color, as were the rooms in Tatiana's house. Silke, though unable to ascend stairs (he lived where the bull used to live, before the bull, growing older, became a nuisance, and was quickly sold), Silke, though unable to raise his arms above his shoulders, had access to all the jars and pots of paint in the small town. He even knew how to prize paint (and other utilities) out of Stefan Triforovitch, should the need be great enough. Heaven had bestowed upon Silke certain compensations—capacities to influence and improvise.

After only a few more days the opera house gleamed like granite; the auditorium dazzled like a flying palace that a child might enter and be never seen on earth again.

"Why do you not wear your yellow boots, Elena Andreievna?" asked Bábaba each morning.

"Because my legs are not yet cold, Bábaba," Elena each morning replied.

The rain had stopped, but the still, dark air was full of suspense as if more than mortal happenings impended.

Elena's own opinion was that she was in a trance, something that happened frequently to girls in *Les coryphées de la petite cave,* for one reason or another. At least one of the girls had drowned herself while in a trance. Another had married a Sergeant of the Guards while in the same condition. Everyone fell into a trance while watching the ballerina spin, leap, and agitate.

Elena had not yet so much as mentioned her opera house to Tatiana, Ismene, Clémence, to Tatiana's Mother, to

Mademoiselle Olivier-Page, or to anyone at all except to Silke, who had only an inexact idea of what Elena was talking about, and helped solely from love of her. No one else in the house had a very clear idea of what Elena was doing at any time. Bábaba might know all that Elena needed to know, but what Elena actually did with herself was another matter.

So far Elena had not told even Mikhail about her opera house, and she was perfectly well aware that this might be significant. She might continue to imply for some time yet, to herself and some others, that Mikhail was perfect, even to do so without a second thought, but she suspected that the brief visit of Herr and Frau Meyrendorff had left her a different person. She resented the prohibition upon her eating the fruit they had brought. The Meyrendorffs' wide knowledge of things had led to their kindly bringing her the strange delicacy at this exact time, directing her to eat the whole of it. Deprived of it, she might well set off in a wrong direction, especially with Bábaba so busy, her Mother so exhausted, and her Father so absent, working to sustain them all. She and Tatiana knew perfectly well that there were precise stages or stopping places in the advance to life's summit, none of them to be omitted without peril.

What spectacle to mount first?

The book offered several possibilities, but Elena decided upon "La Gitana," a ballet interlude to Rossini's best-known opera, because there was only one dancer in it that mattered, and because the dancer wore a red dress.

How bright a red, there could be no precise knowing, but Elena knew just what to do.

Downstairs was a small room which contained, with a few other things, the sad relics of Captain Leonid Gregorovitch Timorasiev, Elena's great-uncle, who had known Lermontov, and had been shot for participating in political activity of some kind. Elena had never taken in all the details, partly because there were stories of that kind about so many men, partly because a much greater impression had been made upon her by the holes in the Captain's azure jacket, each hole still surrounded with a faint brown flush. As well as the jacket, there were carmine breeches, very big boots, and a cap with a dwindled and drooping plume; swords and pistols and wands; a metal traveling box with great-uncle Leonid's full name and rank painted upon the top in white, now grimy with campaigning; and a leather case of great-uncle Leonid's Orders and Decorations. It was upon the last that Elena, on behalf of her opera house, had designs.

She knew exactly what was in the case, because the gorgeous ribbons and swathes had always appealed to her more positively than most other things in the room. It was hard to believe that even so great a man as great-uncle Leonid had been given all this silk by the Tsar, and when, once, she had dared to raise the matter with her Father, her Father had merely smiled and said, "Perhaps not." Visitors to the house, male and female, were always taken to the small room and stood there for moments in total and reverent silence, while Elena's Father watched with concentration for the effect made upon them. One foreign visitor had said he perceived that great-uncle Leonid had been a Freemason.

No one seemed to enter the room unless there were such visitors to the house and now the presentation was often left to Bábaba, who was, at these moments, even more silent than Elena's Father, if that were possible, and who was said actually to have known great-uncle Leonid and to have been his handmaiden. Always someone, after standing his or her few moments, said "Death is beautiful," and always Bábaba then wept, the only time she did.

The room was kept locked, but, equally, the key was kept in the door. Times had been when members of the family wanted to enter the room, privately, and sometimes urgently, in order to brood and meditate there. The assumption was that such times might return. It was no one's part to make that impracticable.

Elena flitted down all the stairs, like a small and intricate flash of lightning, and, within a second, was within the room, with the key accompanying her, and at once used to lock the door on the inside.

That was hardly necessary. It is choice that distinguishes the artist from the common herd, but Elena had known well in advance, had known right from the moment when she had decided which spectacle she was first to present, that there was but one silk in the leather box that would meet her, and her audience's demands, but especially hers. Only her silvery curvaceous scissors were worthy to cut deeply into such a fabric.

Soon the red dress was completed, and Elena had decided that the color was perfect, whatever the Baron de la Touque might have thought; deep and glowing, so that Elena felt drawn right into it, but clear enough also to hold every eye, as Elena confirmed by draping the dress over her wooden pig, setting the pig on top of the stove in her room (not yet lighted, for all Bábaba's talk), and first staring and then squinting at it from the far other side of the room, than which few opera houses could, needless to say, be bigger.

There was pork too for the midday meal, with plenty of unchopped cabbage, and a little cream, though there was only Elena and kind Bábaba to devour it. Bábaba seemed to have stopped grumbling about the need for Elena to feel cold, or about anything else. She was portentously still. Bábaba, like the weather, had an aptitude for implying the future well before it struck.

Elena was packing her book of French verses, her book of simple exercises on the pianoforte (never simple enough for Elena), her small sketching book, and her Young Girl's Realm into the pockets of the plain gray cloak she wore for all ordinary occasions when there was the loudest possible hammer-hammer on the outer door, the imposing front door of the house, not the door through which tradesmen, children, and hens entered. Such a caller should have known the use of the doorbell, at the Timorasiev house singularly conspicuous.

"It must be the Devil," cried Bábaba, still clairvoyant.

Elena crept after her, fascinated, but staying close to the walls.

The caller did not seem like that at all, at least upon first acquaintance. He seemed a jolly fellow. He wore a speckled shirt, striped breeches, and very muddy boots. He had a nose like Punchinello's, big and comic; a face as reddy-brown as that of any peasant in the fields; and remarkably big teeth. His ears projected widely. He laughed all the time he spoke, and as he did so he shimmered and flickered.

Bábaba dismantled the various chains and bars. All the household, and all ordinary people, used the other door. She implied as much with every movement.

"What's *your* name, young man?" asked Bábaba wryly.

Elena was less sure that the visitor was so young. But she knew it to be a matter about which she was often mistaken. She had supposed Mikhail to be forty when he had only been about nineteen!

"Irash," said the man, laughing.

"Is that all?" asked Bábaba suspiciously.

"That is all, old dame, but I have business with Mademoiselle Elena Andreievna Timorasieva. If she is in the house, pray do me the honor of presenting me to her."

The visitor was speaking in Russian, but his accent in the one French word he had used seemed perfectly good, even though he had addressed kind Bábaba so disrespectfully.

Elena slid away from the dark wall.

"I am Elena Andreievna," she said, enunciating most clearly, and almost as if she really were as grown-up as the man's words had implied.

"Mademoiselle!" the visitor exclaimed, as if overwhelmed, and throwing his fur hat to the ground, or rather onto the floor within the house. What was more, he began to speak in French. "Mademoiselle, please conduct me to some private place. I have a gift to bestow."

"Another gift!" cried Elena, not at all like a grown-up.

But, with Elena following, Bábaba led the visitor into the schoolroom: not Elena's schoolroom, of course, but the schoolroom of the sisters of her father, who had once been numerous, and, before them, of their aunts, who had been too many to count, at least by this time. The room now contained nothing but potatoes, some of them gloomily sprouting. Bábaba lurked by the door, curator and chaperon.

The man wasted no time. He fell upon his left knee, bowed before Elena as if she had been a gorgeous Grand Duchess, and was somehow holding out to her a package, with his arms extended above his head and behind his wide ears. It was even more remarkable than Frau von Meyrendorff's presentations because the package was longer and larger. This time, however, it was not wrapped in anything. It was simply a serious wooden box, tied loosely round the middle with undressed hemp.

"Thank you," said Elena, first taking hold of the box

in the middle where the ligature was, but then, realizing its weight, clutching at the two ends with widely parted arms.

"That gift is much too heavy for a child," cried Bábaba, darting forward to take the box from Elena.

"Then I shall carry it upstairs *moi-même,*" said the visitor.

Elena had indeed very nearly dropped the box on her toes, not even protected by boots, as Bábaba had all along recommended. In part, therefore, she was glad to hand it over, though in part apprehensive, having learned by experience what grown-ups so often do with presents returned to their hands.

The visitor dodged past Bábaba as if playing a game, and even Elena managed to elude Bábaba's snatch. Elena had never before felt so light and deft, or never that she could remember. She had not even torn her dress.

The visitor began to leap up the many stairs as if he knew the house like the back of his hat, and as if the box were made of air, which Elena had learned for herself that it certainly was not. Until now, Elena, seldom rampant, except sometimes with Mikhail, would soon have been panting at the pace, but today she was capering upwards like a sprite.

The visitor did not bother with Elena's bedroom, where the book was, but sprang right up to the very top floor and plunged straight into Elena's improvised workshop. He set down the heavy box on the dusty floor.

"Open it now, if you wish," said the visitor politely.

Elena began to pull at the hemp.

"Both hands, mademoiselle," said the visitor, laughing as always.

When the box was opened, Elena saw that it contained jointed wooden figures, neither clothed nor painted. She was used to dolls of that kind, but liked them to look a little brighter. On the other hand, she had never seen so many of them at one time; not even in Ossip Novakov's workshop. With the eye of an artist Elena could see that the dolls in the box varied in stature and shape, though only a little.

"Thank you very much," said Elena. "They will make a platoon of soldiers." She knew that this was always the procedure when many people were available, all looking more or less alike. The Tsar himself required it.

"*Mais non,* mademoiselle," said the visitor, laughing more noticeably than ever. "Think again, if you please. Look again. Consider further."

"Oh!" cried Elena. "Oh!"

"They are not soldiers," said the visitor, "but *coryphées*. Perhaps you do not know that word?"

At this moment Bábaba struggled in, wheezing like a bellows, and deep red all over, if one might judge by her visible face and two hands. She had quite possibly never mounted before as high in the house. Bábaba had other things to do than climb stairs without end in search of children without respect.

"Oh, go away, Bábaba," cried Elena, in great excitement, before Bábaba had been able to say one word.

Bábaba all but burst with exertion and indignity.

"Go away, Bábaba," repeated Elena, so eager to continue with her real life.

It could have been predicted that Bábaba would cease trying for words. She seized the stout stick that stood in the corner of the makeshift workroom. Elena's brothers used it for killing ducks.

But the visitor stepped towards her.

"Pray descend, madame," he said in a soft but firm voice, smiling enigmatically.

Elena had already noticed for herself that the visitor's good manners were not exactly those of a professional messenger. Moreover, there was normally one person only in the house to be addressed as madame.

Make what one might of such factors, true it was that Bábaba first put the stout stick back in its place, then cast her eyes floorwards, then quietly shuffled from the *soi-disant* workplace. She had not uttered one single word. It was something else that Elena had never before seen.

The visitor struck an attitude.

"*Coryphées,*" said the visitor, his yellow eyes glinting, his hairy finger pointing, his toes angled.

"Yes," said Elena. "I should have known."

The visitor merely waited for Elena to speak again. He had never been so completely still since he had entered the house, never before for two seconds.

"They will all need dresses," said Elena anxiously. But it was important not to be overwhelmed.

"No doubt," said the visitor. It was just when one might have expected his laughter to become positively boisterous, but Elena distinctly noticed that he was not even smiling.

"I have woven a dress for the ballerina," said Elena.

"Woven?"

Elena blushed. "Sewed," she said.

"It is the right red, of course?"

Elena nodded. She had no means of knowing. She looked hard at the contents of the box.

"Which is the ballerina?" she asked.

"You are the ballerina," said the visitor.

As he spoke, the rain began to fall again, and there was a ripple of thunder. Elena knew it was essential to behave quite naturally. Maturity was astalk.

"I'm too big," said Elena, smiling in turn.

"This is a small town," said the visitor.

Elena nodded again. Everyone remarked upon how small a town it was.

"What can I do?" Elena asked.

"You must come to Smorevsk. More room. More people. I shall await you. Remember that my name is Irash."

"I shall die before forgetting that," said Elena, very seriously.

After, through another of the dirty windows, she had watched the visitor springing down the empty street in his fur hat, dodging all the many puddles, almost dodging the separate columns of rain; after she had seen him lose shape, diminish, and vanish: after these experiences, Elena decided in an instant that a model was one thing, her own life another.

If she were to be a ballerina in Smorevsk, and surely as soon as possible, it was hardly worthwhile spending difficult hours in making her spangled blue curtain rise and fall, or far more difficult days and weeks making dresses for her entire troupe: dressmaking being one further art in which Elena fully realized that, alas, she would never graduate—or even truly participate. Elena glanced dubiously at the timbery horde. For a task of that magnitude she would have had to enroll Tatiana and the rest, which would have meant revealing almost everything, which would almost certainly have been a mistake, though Elena had little idea why it should be. It was simply a lesson she had learned.

Ismene's Grandmother's companion, an elderly lady from Azerbaijan, understood to have been once a slave, frequently referred to life's lessons, and to their importance, especially to females, who had so few other opportunities to learn anything.

Elena put the lid on the box and slowly descended the stairs. It was impossible to decide what to do for the best, to decide before it was time for the next meal (whether or not the next meal appeared on time). Elena supposed that the model she had built, with only Silke's aid, must offer guidance of some kind, if only the guidance could be interpreted. Something was bound to happen because she was still young.

In the meantime Elena withdrew quietly to her bedroom and seated herself on the floor, turning over the pages of her new book, as if she had been a monk with his Virgil. The rug beneath her had been looted years before from a British Asiatic station by men under the command of one of Elena's many relatives who had died or disappeared heroically. When much younger, Elena had often used the rug to disguise herself as an Indian elephant.

The trouble with life's monitions was that, though leading to action, they were often so intrinsically unpleasant; nor did the book say otherwise, not for one moment. Elena read with new attention the account of a girl who had married a handsome student without realizing that he was really a convicted criminal, escaped only a few weeks before from a party set to digging up beetroot. The poor girl had to live through the experience of her husband being ultimately guillotined for murdering their innocent, but starving, child. Elena's eyes had previously slid over the tale. At least, she now reflected, there was no guillotine in Holy Russia. All the same, Elena shuddered.

That same afternoon Elena's Mother asked to see her. The message was brought to Elena by no less an unexpected person than Cook, hiccoughing the while, as always. Bábaba still refused to speak to Elena, or to see her feed, or to set eyes on her, or to listen to any apologies, had apologies been even offered.

Elena tapped at the discolored door.

"Mamma!"

Standing instructions were that there was never to be any shock to poor Mamma's nerves; not even if fire broke out, as it sometimes did.

"Mamma!"

"Enter, Elena."

Mamma was actually out of bed and seated in a quilted gown before the stove, with kerosene heaters ranged round her chair, as satellites round a planet. The clockwork machine had been turned off, or left unwound.

"Sit down, Elena. I hope you have been good."

"Oh, yes, Mamma."

Elena seated herself on a small black stool. The other seats in the room were to the rear of the great chair. Most of them were never sat upon because never was more than one visitor admitted at a time, or never more than one who could be invited to be seated. Elena's stool stood beneath a large and realistic engraving of Alexandra Alexandrevna Alexandrova: Elena's Mother's Great-aunt, who, after years of humility, had finally been beatified. The heads of innocent children surrounded her, all rather alike. No doubt they were cherubim.

"I trust that you have been working hard at all your lessons, Elena."

"Of course, Mamma. Mademoiselle Olivier-Page gives us no respite. But how are *you,* Mamma? How are your sufferings?"

"It is the decree of God, Elena, that they are to continue."

Elena's Mother crossed herself, and waited for Elena to do the same.

"I grieve, Mamma."

"Ah! That is why I have sent for you, Elena."

"It is always a delight to visit you, Mamma." That phrase was something that Elena had indeed learned from Mademoiselle Olivier-Page, who used it on many occasions.

"Elena!" Her Mother cried out in a deep and stirring voice. Her huge, faded eyes, set above faded cheeks, gazed at Elena through dependent, faded locks.

"Mamma, yes, what is it?" Elena, soft-hearted by nature, and soft-hearted still, was affected. She extended one hand a certain distance.

"Elena, have you considered committing yourself to the life of religion?"

"No," said Elena.

"Last night, only last night," said Elena's Mother, softly and magnetically, "I had a vision of God. God himself said to me that a sacrifice was needed. A sacrifice to Him."

"Needed for what, Mamma?" Elena had for some days been thinking of things so very different, and at nights also.

"For my recovery, Elena. For what else?" Now the faded eyes were glowing redly, as if the stove had been open, the faded hairs beginning to gleam and stiffen.

"I see, Mamma. I'm sorry I didn't understand."

"But you understand now, Elena."

"Do I, Mamma?"

"It is the only way. God has spoken directly to me, and has told me this."

Elena longed to take off her dress, to take off more than her dress: or, if that were impossible, to jump through the window, to run until she dropped insensible, to seek reassurance of Tatiana, of Ismene, even of pretty, gifted Clémence, who looked for a witty joke in everything.

"Oh, Mamma."

All the same: Elena knew that here was another occasion when it was necessary to behave quite naturally; not for a moment to lose all hold. Two occasions in a single day!

"Will you cease to live except for sacrifice, Elena?"

"No." This time Elena shook her head, reinforcing herself, since there was no one else to do it.

All the time, from far below, one could hear Asmara coughing out her lungs, her heart, her life.

"Will you spurn all wiles? Will you live as if dead?"

It was as if Elena had never uttered, let alone so definitively.

"For your Mother's sake? For your own sake? For the sake of God?"

Now the eyes were like braziers, and the whole being luminous.

"I want to marry and have children, Mamma, as many children as Frau von Meyrendorff."

The words had leapt out regardless of all the sad miscarriages and stillbirths. Elena would have flushed upon the instant, and very deeply, had the room not been so hot already. Hastily she put forward an alternative ambition.

"I want to be a ballerina, Mamma, like Frau von Meyrendorff's book."

"Letitia von Schaden was a loose girl. Married, she is a light woman. She has left this house for good."

"Why was that, Mamma? She promised to come and see me, and she didn't."

"That is what we all learned to expect of Letitia von Schaden. One day she was caught trying to cheat at Greek; another day substituting something she had bought for something she should have made."

"Then why have we gone on knowing her at all, Mamma?"

Elena was deeply relieved by the change in the subject of conversation; so unplanned, but so easily brought about. The Baron, referring to one of his girls, had written of the volatility and changefulness often displayed by invalids. It was as if Elena had never read any other book, nor needed to.

[43]

"There is such a thing as loyalty, Elena. You are too young to know about it."

Elena realized that the conversational cockleshell was again being borne towards turbulent waters.

"Tell me about Greek, Mamma."

"It is very like Russian, Elena, but has only half the letters."

"Say something in Greek, Mamma!"

Γυναῖκα γὰρ δὴ συμπονεῖν γυναικὶ χρή.

"What does it mean, Mamma?"

"It means, Elena, that we women should stand together. It was the motto of the school."

It was the very first time that Elena's Mamma had spoken of Elena as a woman! Or referred in so many words to the school, let alone to its motto!

"Without a sacrifice I am doomed, Elena. God has told me."

"May I have time to think about it, Mamma?"

It was the form of words used by Ismene when people asked her to do anything much but hang from the parallel bars or rafters or the new girders; grown-up people, naturally.

"You must not only think, Elena. You must pray." Elena's Mother smiled very sweetly but very sadly. She was smiling at Elena, but also at life, or at least at the room as a whole.

She spoke again.

"Thinking is not always for the best, Elena." Now

Elena's Mother's eyes were full of memories. "I am reminded of something else in Greek. τὸ αὐτόματον ἡμῶν καλλίω βουλεύεται. Chance contrives better for us than we do for ourselves."

"Yes, Mamma. I know it does."

Elena was quite overcome by the truth of the words. Lately, she had received proof of it every day, sometimes more than once in a day. No words, she knew, could be more important. It was astonishing that someone else had noticed what she had noticed, and so long ago: since when it all had been forgotten. It would be a mistake, however, to disclose more than she could help, especially in the exact circumstances.

But her Mother seemed to notice few of Elena's disclosures.

"That was said by Menander," said her Mother.

"And the motto, Mamma?"

"By Euripides, Elena. He sympathized warmly with the plight of all women."

"Warmly, Mamma?"

But her Mother, like most people, was adhering to her own deep insights and purposes.

"Chance, Elena, has always to be aided by prayer. That is what we Christians have added to the knowledge of the Greeks. That is what religion means."

It has also been said, almost certainly by another Greek, that wonders seldom cease. Remedies are another matter.

That very same evening Elena's Father returned early from the Court.

He came upon Stefan Triforovitch sawing up old furniture from the big outhouse, once the cow shed, because there was nothing else left to saw. Vodka in a jug stood upon a desk turned upon its side; or the nearest thing to vodka that the law allowed to be made at home, perhaps a little nearer.

"Blessings be upon you, Andrei Alexeitch."

"And upon you, Stefan Triforovitch."

"I am worn with toil, Andrei Alexeitch," continued Stefan, taking a swig from the homely jar.

"And I, Stefan Triforovitch. I work by day and by night to sustain all of you. It is the decree of God."

Elena's Father entered the house through the door used by tradesmen, children, and hens, and by ordinary people too. He went straight to his room and after ten or twelve minutes with the clubs, and another eight or ten in a cold bath (always kept filled in readiness), he dressed somewhat less formally than usual, descended to his study, and called for Bábaba.

"Ask my daughter, Elena, to come to me here."

It was the most direct of orders, and from the master of the house, so that Bábaba, for all she had endured, could scarcely jib, or not overtly.

But, to deliver the message, she chose the fewest words possible: proper names apart. Elena was mooching up and down, conscious that it was impossible to decide what to do for the best, longing for chance to show its hand sooner than seemed likely, certain only that sacrifice was not the solution, that the moment was premature for sacrifice of any kind.

"Elena Andreievna, go to your Father, Andrei Alexeitch."

Elena tapped at the study door.

"Is that Elena?"

"Yes, Papa."

Elena's Father did not tell her to enter but opened the door for her, as if she had been a ballerina already or at least the wife of the Military Governor.

"Sit down, Elena. On the divan, if you like."

"Thank you, Papa," said Elena, curtsying slightly.

The divan had been brought by artillerymen from near Peshawar.

"How lovely you already are, Elena!" said her Father, stealing a glance at her, as he walked up and down.

Elena thought it best simply to smile. Not being a little donkey, she knew quite well that Tatiana was more beautiful than she, and perhaps Clémence also, being French;

[47]

though things might well be different when she, Elena, was a ballerina, which might well be soon. A simple smile was all that would compass these complexities.

"You are already more lovely than your Mother ever was," said Elena's Father, in something of a mutter, as he paced. Elena had begun to sprawl a little.

"Oh no, Papa."

Her Father shot another quick glance at her.

"I am in an exalted state," he said. "But never mind that."

"But of course I mind, Papa. We all mind."

"It is the uncertainty of my work. The Courts are torture chambers. Never look to the law for a living, Elena. A lawyer receives neither thanks nor payment, neither honors nor kopecks."

"Women are not permitted to be lawyers, Papa." Elena had that afternoon been given express license to be a woman as well as a girl, and a woman she would soon have to be, she supposed, as things were going. Undoubtedly, it was a drawback. She realized too that there would be other demands.

"Women are protected from it, Elena," said Papa, smiling sadly but proudly, though looking straight before him, so that it was difficult to decide whether he was thinking of Elena in particular. He was striding up and down the room, stepping elegantly from the hips, as he always did, often quite unconsciously.

"Women are better suited to the arts, Papa," volunteered Elena, though, as a matter of fact, Mademoiselle Olivier-Page had once said the exact opposite, that, hélas, there was no female Racine, or Rameau, or David. Elena and the others could for the present only wonder whether this was true, and, if so, why?

"That is very correct," said Elena's Papa, indulgently. "Therefore, I have for you a plan, little Elena, though it cannot instantly mature in full." He turned on his heel as he spoke. "Nonetheless, it will offer something to look forward to."

"What is the plan, Papa?" For a third time in one single day she was being called upon to act quite normally, to show no sign of anything in particular.

"It will secure your entire future, Elena."

"What is the plan, Papa?"

Suddenly, her Father ceased to pace and turn. He fell almost on his knees by the divan, as if he were pleading with Elena for some immense necessity. He began to speak even faster and more nervously than he usually did.

"You have heard me speak of Count and Countess Wilmarazov-Totin?"

"No, Papa."

"Ah," he cried, "I try to keep my melancholy affairs concealed from you all, even though you live by them."

"Tell me, Papa," said Elena, though a little cautiously.

"They owe me more rubles than would fill one of the

Emperor's largest ammunition wagons. I do not know how many rubles."

"You must take them to Court, Papa."

"I have done so, little Elena. I have already ruined all of us by doing it."

"How can that possibly be, Papa?"

"It is the fatal beauty of the Countess. It is time that you began to hear of such things. The Divisional Judge is an old man, old, old." Elena's Father tore his hair for a moment.

Elena considered. "But what is the plan, Papa?"

Her Father began to stare at her face with the utmost concentration available to him. His eyes were a trifle glaucous, even fishy. Former sportsmen often have such eyes. There has ceased to be a ball or a bird or other small, distant object upon which their gaze can concentrate.

"Count Wilmarazov is of a great family and Countess Totin of a greater. That told against me in Court also. Such is our life."

"You come of a fine family too, Papa. We all do." Elena lowered her legs to the floor, in order to concentrate better.

"Do you know what the old man's judgment was? He must be ninety-one, or ninety-two. He decided that the Count and Countess owed nothing because the advice I had given them was faulty, and the line of action I had followed on their behalf was misconceived. As if one has to be a Solomon or a Father Stelakovski in order to be a provincial lawyer! Not in all history have such judgments been directed at any lawyer but me!"

"Oh, Papa," said Elena.

"I was ordered to pay and to repay thousands of rubles. I do not know how many. I am probably ruined, Elena. It is all but certain."

"Oh!" cried Elena.

But her Father continued to emit words at her as if he had been alone in the room with his soul. Elena thought it best to avert her eyes from his for a short time.

"The Count took me aside. There is a little room at the Court for such purposes. Despairing men and women have blown their brains out there, or hanged themselves. Madmen have written on the walls. I feel these things every time I enter that room. The Count is of a great family, Elena, the Countess of a family greater still. The Count offered to set me free, to secure my honor, to save me from all immediate burdens, if you, Elena, would go each day as a companion to his son, Rurik. A carriage would call for you, with a footman, and a different carriage would bring you back. The nearest of the Count's manor houses is less than twelve versts distant, and sometimes you could stay the night there. I need not detail to you, Elena, the prospects that might ultimately offer. You are by now quite sufficiently grown-up to see some of them for yourself. Rurik is the Count's only son, and therefore his heir; indeed his only child, owing to the Countess suffering from a malady of some kind, which takes her much out of our country, and prevents her being able to look after children. Rurik is so highly strung that he is in danger from the situation. The Count says that a lovely girl of the right age is a necessity, and that his choice very naturally fell upon you, though he saw you only at your lessons, and then only through the open window. Aren't you pleased by such a compliment, Elena?"

"No," said Elena.

"Then you cannot be a woman!" exclaimed her Father, without really thinking.

Elena clung to natural behavior, to holding on to herself, to showing no signs. Perhaps it was all becoming easier with this constant practice.

"The Count has simply made a mistake," she said. "It was Tatiana he saw, or even Clémence. I am by no means so lovely as they are."

Her Father, still with his legs beneath him on the floor, stared at her for more than a moment. Elena could see her suggestion descending like a lozenge. But her Father recovered like the sportsman he once had been.

"It is no matter if something of that is true," he rejoined, but more slowly. "It is for you that the Count has asked. For you, by your name. Do you not see what a wonderful opportunity opens before you, to snatch good from evil?"

"No," said Elena.

"Do you not feel compassion for Rurik?"

"I do not know, Papa."

"Do you not see a thousand possibilities in one?"

"I don't think so, Papa."

Her Father sprang to his feet like a cheetah who has been molested.

"Do you care so little for your Father?"

"I love you, Papa, and I always shall."

"Love requires sacrifice, Elena."

Elena said nothing.

"I may not be able to look after you always."

"I hope that will not be necessary, Papa. I am sure that it will not."

"You are asked only to sport with Rurik. He asks only to sport with you."

"I have playmates already, Papa."

"But you haven't even seen Rurik?"

"Clémence saw him once, Papa."

Her Father began again to pace, trimly as a generation ago.

"Suppose I die of debt?"

"You are far too athletic ever to die of anything, dear Papa."

"Suppose I die of your ingratitude, Elena?"

So there was little alternative to Elena setting out for Smorevsk as soon as possible.

Of course there were farewells to come first, however provisional.

Partir, c'est mourir un peu.

Every time it was true, though Elena had decided there should be only three times.

From these three persons news of her departure (for the time being) would reach everyone else. She also thought that these three might understand things.

When the time came, it was hard to say whether or not they did.

Tatiana had been asked by Elena to come back to the Timorasiev house after their lessons. Now they were in Elena's big bedroom, and Tatiana was weeping wildly. The book lay rejected on the rug, and Elena's further explanation had gone for nothing. Elena was afraid that Tatiana might become demented and do one of them, or perhaps someone else, a mischief.

Silke, to whom less could be elucidated, but by whom more was divined, neither wept or protested nor did he attempt to dissuade.

"I shall never see you again, Elena Andreievna," he asserted with finality.

"Of course you will, Silke. I could never manage anything without you."

With Mikhail, Elena was walking down one of the muddy, misty roads that lead nowhere.

"You are too young to do this, Elena."

"The book says not and Irash said I was a ballerina already."

"That is absurd, Elena."

"I have no choice, Mikhail Mikhailovitch."

"Endure for a few more years and then marry me, Elena. It was always what we planned. Then we shall go away, but together."

"I may come back and do that, Mikhail Mikhailovitch."

"Waking and sleeping I think only of you, Elena. All that I do is for you. All that I am."

"I know, Mikhail Mikhailovitch."

He began to sing. The music of the song was traditional, fifty or a hundred years old at least, but the words were original.

> *A sparrow came to me and said,*
> *Love.*
> *A blackbird came to me and said,*
> *Love on.*

A swallow came to me and said,
  Love now.
An eagle came to me saying,
  Love forever.
A flashing, darting parakeet said
  Love.
A pigeon queen of all the words said,
  Love afar.
A hooting, melting, moulting owl said,
  Love at night.
A lovebird, pink and blue, came whispering,
  I am love.

But Mikhail had left behind his balalaika because Elena that day had seemed so serious; and now the mist was filling his throat, so that he was compelled to stop, because it was essential to close his mouth. Weathermen might by now have called it fog.

So winter seemed nearer than ever, and it was essential for Elena to reach Smorevsk before it arrived. After all, she did not wish to join the unnamed multitude who each year simply died on the roads. The three to whom she had spoken had thus far kept silent, as she had made each of them swear to do; but the oath expired as soon as she was gone, and it would be unwise to expect too much, especially of Tatiana, who had almost immediately taken to her bed with a low fever, and was living exclusively on skimmed goats' milk and gelatin.

The road to Smorevsk was at least believed to go there, and Elena had met people who had been there or come from there along it, Irash presumably of the number; but to Elena it looked, in the fog, much like any other road, but perhaps a little less frequented. Many people might find it discouraging that there was no community for seventy-two versts. Elena had little idea of what there could be for seventy-two versts. The railroad, in every way superlative, did not go to Smorevsk, only to some vague unknown place in the south. Wearing her gray winter tunic and skirt for the first time that autumn, her ordinary gray cloak, and her gray fur hat, Elena stepped out strongly. She would have liked to appear in Smorevsk wearing her green velvet cloak, but, fingering its thickness, and rubbing her cheek against its pile, she had realized that it was more for receptions than for excursions. She might be able to send someone back for it when she was a ballerina. In any case, it would still of course fit her when she returned from Smorevsk, as she planned. As things were, she was missing Tatiana at every step, and Mikhail whenever she thought about him.

The very first living thing that Elena encountered in

the fog (or the very first living thing that was large enough to be seen) was a bear. It was standing in the very middle of the mud as if it were waiting for her. As far as Elena could tell it was a brown bear, but she had never before seen a bear out of captivity, often very mournful captivity. Elena emitted a slight shriek, which was immediately strangled by the fog, and then called upon her now almost habitual recourse of calm, normality, and absence of all feeling, as with ordinary people.

"Hullo," said Elena.

The bear seemed to smile, as far as the shape of its features permitted, and then shambled towards Elena like a dog, and began to snuffle round her ankles and the bottom of her skirt. Probably it sought sustenance, but Elena had none to spare. On so long a journey she could not burden herself with tidbits for every random quadruped. She patted the bear a little dubiously on the head, at which the bear began to slaver over her boots.

Elena might well have walked on because no one could claim that the bear was blocking her path, but she hesitated. Perhaps it really was time for her first soupçon? Ismene's Father, on almost the only occasion she had been alone with him, had told her how important it was that men on the march be fed small amounts frequently. He had remarked upon it, even though he himself was in the police—in two kinds of police. Elena seated herself on a stone and ate two radishes and half a slice of rich cake. Though it would be necessary to conserve supplies, she offered the bear a radish. It was the largest radish in the sack, but the bear refused it, with a short bark, so that the radish fell in the mud and was spoiled, unless for cooking. The bear then ambled away, looking disappointed, and was almost immediately lost to sight in the fog, for all its bulk.

Elena's next encounter was with an old, gray woman, far grayer than anyone Elena had previously ever seen. (Elena herself was of course dressed in gray, but that was another matter.) The old woman was spare as a gray reed. She stared straight before her, but Elena wondered whether she saw anything at all. In both her hands were gray bones. Elena could not decide what kind of bones they were because the woman was on her way with them almost as soon as Elena had sighted her. The woman's legs were like broomsticks, thrusting and fatless.

Then Elena was overtaken by a coach. She had heard rumblings for some little time but had supposed them to be caused by marsh gases. The coach proved to be drawn by four horses, as like one another as beans, black beans; all of which was unusual in Elena's small town, where most people had to take what they could get. What was more, the coach was being followed by a whole pack of wolflike dogs, all groomed and glistening, though possibly with exertion and vapor from the atmosphere.

The coach stopped and the sleek, moist dogs clustered round it and Elena like waterweed. Elena felt a thrill of fear. This might well be Count Wilmarazov-Totin, on the way to one of his manors; or even the frightful goblin, Rurik, for whom a partner in sport had to be purchased and paid for—if anyone were rich enough, which of course no one was.

The coach window descended with a crash, and a strange head obtruded. Again, Elena had seen nothing like it, but she had no idea what Count Wilmarazov-Totin looked like.

"Mademoiselle, would you care for a ride?"

The voice was high and chanting, and the words almost those of a song. However, the accent was purity itself.

"I don't think so," said Elena, who was never a little goose. "I have made my own plans." That was another useful expression which Elena had picked up from someone or other.

Elena courteously but concisely added, "Thank you very much."

The high voice uttered again. "One hour ahead, the road is blocked by dragoons. You will not be permitted to pass, and you will be in mortal danger."

Elena considered. She saw that she must at all costs make a calm and rational decision. "Are you going to one of your manors?" she inquired.

"I no longer possess manors, mademoiselle. I have sold them all and abandoned everything."

"Why?" asked Elena instantly.

"For the cause of freedom."

"For freedom?" cried Elena. "Then you are not Count Wilmarazov-Totin?"

"I shall simply observe that I am sure you do not know what you ask."

"No," said Elena. "I don't." She wanted to say no more, nor to think more, of Count Wilmarazov-Totin or of his appalling family, so, in order to say something, she remarked, "I am under a spell," which she believed to be nothing but the truth.

By now Elena had realized that this host of dogs was strange too. It was as if they were waiting for an order, and could do nothing without one.

"Where is the spell taking you?" asked the strange man.

"To Smorevsk, where I am to be a ballerina."

"You are a *coryphée!!*" cried the strange man in a voice higher than ever, far higher. "You are lost in dreams!"

"No, I am not lost," said Elena, smiling as she stood amid the silent, motionless dogs.

The strange man was trying to open the carriage door himself, instead of waiting for the footman to leap down and do it. In any case, the footman sat stolidly on the box, looking like a toad. The coachman looked a little different: more like a frog.

"Let me help," said Elena, politely grasping the big outside handle of unpolished brass, and giving it the sharpest wrench she could. She realized that the man would have wished to hurl the door open for her with a single fling. To things like that she must now accustom herself, and to gracious helpfulness when they did not occur.

"Enter!" said the man, now a little more reserved after the episode of the door. "For you my coach is floored with cloth of gold."

Before shutting the window he hung out once more and shouted to his retainers as if to a droshky driver in Petersburg: "To the Opera, and hurry."

The coach began to rumble on; not particularly fast, Elena thought. But then the floor was not of gold cloth. It was of bare damp wood, which Elena thought might easily be rotten in places. There were probably worms and slugs creeping round her boots all the time. She looked out. The dogs were hardly needing to trot.

"I must present myself," said the strange man. "I am Prince Alexei Vladimirovitch Popelevski. I am the Patron of the Smorevsk Opera. It is a hereditary position, one among many."

"Oh!" said Elena, regardless of all rules.

"I am usually addressed as Lexi. Will you do that?"

"I shall try," said Elena, a little doubtfully.

"I am a strange person," said Lexi.

"I thought you were," said Elena.

"I am at once everything, and nothing."

"I have a friend like that. He is called Mikhail."

Lexi looked away from Elena for a moment. "He is a young boy?"

Elena laughed, which until recently she would never have been able to do. "He is a man. He is more than twenty."

"Tell me about him."

"Mikhail looks like a Grand Duke. He writes poems. He paints pictures. He sings in the fields and roads. There is nothing he cannot do. Or not many things."

"Do you love him?"

"I am too young," said Elena, thus meeting the external and the internal situation with the same words.

"Is he following you to Smorevsk?"

"No. I told him not to."

"So he is distraught?"

"Of course not. Soon I shall go back."

"You will never go back. You will go on."

Elena looked at him closely for the first time. She decided that the upper half of his face was masculine, the lower half feminine. It would be unwise, therefore, to rely upon every word he said.

"I may be marrying Mikhail."

"Ballerinas can marry only their business managers."

"I read a book that said something like that."

"Marriage is for *coryphées.*"

"Yes, the book said that too."

"Marriage is not for all, mademoiselle. I shall never marry."

"Why ever not?"

"Would you care for a *marron glacé*?"

"Thank you."

It was as big as a beetle and had much the same texture.

"Prince Popelevski," began Elena, with her mouth full.

"Do not call me that."

"I am too young to treat you with familiarity."

Lexi leaned across the coach, and, even though his mouth was full also, kissed her energetically.

"So much for familiarity," he intoned.

Elena remained calm. She looked out of her window for a moment at the slowly passing mud. The *marron* was stuck at the top of her throat, at once gluey and scratchy.

She glanced back at Lexi. He was by no means following up his assault with the wild words and mad further actions of which Elena had both heard and read (at times, Tatiana spoke of little else). He was plunged back in his corner, gnawing convulsively, and quivering to excess. Elena felt very nearly sorry for him. Plainly it would be wiser not to address him by name of any kind. She succeeded in extricating the sweetmeat from her pharynx.

"How do you manage to feed all these dogs?" No question could be more natural. It was also the question she had intended in the first place.

"They are ancestors. They are all that is left. They cannot leave me. They need no feeding."

"Do you mean that they are only ghost dogs?"

"Simple people might call them that. Birs and Fors do need feeding. You have seen them on the box. They are unemancipated serfs."

"But that is impossible! All the serfs are emancipated."

"Birs and Fors refused. They are obdurate and stupid. They contribute little but they refuse to be freed. They eat heavily."

Elena looked through the forward ornamental glasswork at the two bottoms, each wide as a wall, or wider. The ripple of the moving jaws ran through the two frames.

"Which is which?"

"I forget."

They came to the place where the dragoons were blocking the road.

"Why do they do it?" asked Elena, as she peeked at the wild faces and copious whiskers through the mist.

"They are under orders," said Lexi.

He was beginning to brandish his credentials, as the motion of the carriage slowly subsided.

The noncommissioned officer in charge of the posse, portlier than the rest and even more hairy, passed the documents to a young recruit who could read. The recruit explained as best he could to the noncommissioned officer what was in the documents. The noncommissioned officer gave the recruit a playful, but manly, cuff, and took the documents back. The recruit, as he reeled sideways, kept his eyes away from Elena's eyes, she being not so very different in age. The noncommissioned officer saluted, though perhaps a little less formally than he would have done to the Emperor, and in no time the cortege was on its way once more, with no lives lost or tears shed.

"Who *gives* the orders?" asked Elena.

"It is the way we are ruled," said Lexi.

Elena inquired no further.

The cortege, equine, human, spectral, stumbled endlessly on through the eternal fog. No one overtook them though it would not have been difficult. No one came toward them either. Elena and Lexi nibbled delicacies and crudities alternately. Every now and then the horses had to be stoked up and watered. This was done by stopping at some place where more than the usual quantity of liquid had broken through to the surface, and then distributing feed in battered round cans bearing the Popelevski insignia, which was entwined dragons. The feed was sometimes augmented by produce from the land, harvested by Birs and Fors in their distorting topcoats and obliterating headgear. They chewed as they plucked.

On the first night they stayed in the castle of an old Countess, who was mad, and invisible, though audible. Elena found the hours of darkness unpredictable.

On the second night their host was a Baron, bluff and booming, though unable to paint or play or sing or read or write, as Elena soon detected. All his servants were men, but they wore no liveries. Many of them hardly wore clothes. Lexi had told Elena, before their arrival, that the Baron had beaten several wives to death because they had failed to give birth to boys, but that now he had undergone a medical operation on his brain and had lost all interest in women. Such things were perfectly possible with all the new discoveries, including devices for making people insensible while the things were done to them. Nonetheless Elena suspected that it was the Baron who battered at her door for hours (as it seemed) during the long damp darkness. Elena had shot the heavy wooden bolts, and turned both locks, and driven in several wedges intended for something else; so she simply waited for the din to stop, which in the end it did, though the door was too thick for her to hear retreating feet or boots. Earlier she had noticed that the Baron's brutal-looking dogs had withdrawn shrieking from Lexi's dogs. It had given her confidence.

"How would you have fared for accommodation, mademoiselle, if you had been unprotected?" asked Lexi, as they rumbled away from the Baron's establishment. Like the Countess's castle, it had indeed stood far from the highway, and could never have been spotted by the naked eye at dusk in the almost permanent fog.

"I had made my own plans," replied Elena smiling.

She had noticed that Lexi had never yet asked her name. She supposed this to be because a ballerina's real name is unimportant. Lexi had also begun to smoke, exactly as if Elena had been a male comrade. Soon the air was thick.

Despite what she had said, Elena fully realized how advantageous it was to be traveling with a person who could call upon friends for a bed or beds almost anywhere in Russia.

[67]

"It was very kind of you to help me," said Elena from quite deep down.

"I am part of your spell," Lexi chanted back.

Elena nodded. She looked at him again. This time, she fancied that the top part of his face was feminine, the lower part masculine. People's constitutions changed with their moods, or with the tides, as did their dependability.

"Who is Irash?" inquired Elena.

"The most perfect fellow," replied Lexi. "The most perfect fellow you'll ever meet."

"He gave me a box of dancers, with jointed legs and arms."

"Do not tire them."

Elena had, in fact, carefully packed the box away under all the boxes of tools, and under the model in another box.

"If you are the Patron of the Opera," she persisted, "what is Irash?"

"He is the creative genius, mademoiselle. It is always useless to have an opera, and no creative genius. It is a mistake commonly made."

Lexi was puffing steadily, filling the coach with almost black smoke.

Elena was not to be deflected. It was the personal aspect that counted, as with everybody. She, a star rising with immense rapidity, was alone in a coach with the Patron of the Opera, and him half-intoxicated with nicotine.

"Will Irash teach me to dance better than the others?"

"If you are in Irash's hands, you will need no tuition, mademoiselle. Irash is creative, not didactic. Perhaps you do not know the meaning of those words."

What Lexi had said seemed very surprising, but at that exact point something began to stir within Elena, as something had begun to stir when she had been seated with her eyes on the spotty ceiling and the bucket of bulletty cherries between her legs. What was stirring now, Elena had no idea, any more than on the earlier occasion. The future could be depended upon to disclose.

"What does Irash do at the Opera, and what do you do?"

"I am responsible for everything and nothing. I am the mere titular deity. Irash creates, directs, exalts."

"I don't really understand," said Elena, after careful thought.

"In art there is very little definition, mademoiselle."

"But don't I *need* to understand?" asked Elena.

"Not at all, mademoiselle. Only to trust."

"Trust who, Lexi? Trust Irash?"

She had actually used Lexi's name, and quite without forethought.

"You have an inner voice, mademoiselle. Or shall we say, a Muse? Irash heard it call, or no doubt you would not be here in my carriage. He will enable you to do as it bids. It is your true self that you must trust."

[69]

"Ah!" said Elena. It was all so contrary to familiar teachings, and to Bábaba's in particular.

But now the cavern of Lexi's big pipe glowed like the bowl of Elburz or Etna. The floor of the coach was being strewn with fiery particles, which instantly died as the damp struck them. The air was hot and strong. A portent from Heaven was the least that could have been expected, had the atmosphere outside been clearer.

"I *think* I understand," said Elena, cautiously.

"There is no doubt about it," squeaked Lexi, holding in the smoke for a moment, like a conjuror.

And then there *was* a portent. Suddenly, everything, inside and outside, was bright sunshine, and the Gates of Smorevsk were visible, only two versts away, across the peat bog.

Mist and fog can be very local in their distribution, especially in mid-autumn.

Within the coach, Elena felt much too hot, as if her Mother had been there.

Above the gates were the usual ghastly heads on spikes, which no one ever quite knew when to remove. Around the gates, and depending from the walls, sometimes hardly less dexterously than Ismene, were people of all colors, all costumes, all languages, all purposes. No effort was being made to protect them from one another, or even from themselves.

Lexi had no trouble in signifying either his rank or his position. Elena noticed that the big gates were stuck down and rusted. Probably they had not been closed for years and years, whatever the regulation might be. Security was in the hands of the gatemen, who were covered with ornamental knives and antique pistols from shoulder to knee. Here too, Elena wondered how she would have fared, had she emerged footsore and without papers. She was much too young to have papers, besides being a female.

The streets were crowded with charlatans, mountebanks, and nursemaids. There was a samovar at every corner, either steaming or being mended. The thousand churches tinkled their bells gloriously, as if to welcome the new ballerina; the gold decorations everywhere flashed in the sun; the multicolored doves swooped and wheeled and purred. Elena did not know whether there really were a thousand churches, but it seemed likely. Everything was completely different from her own small town.

Birs and Fors were imbibing now, as well as munching, and singing too, though less blithely than Mikhail, and neither in unison nor in harmony. The dogs plodded engagingly, as if still crossing the boundless fens, even though none of the populace seemed to see them, let alone make way for them. Every now and then a young officer of dragoons galloped past with a message. Each one of them either saluted Lexi or waved gaily to him, and in some cases, there was time for Elena to bow slightly.

"Dear Smorevsk!" murmured Lexi, knocking out his pipe on the underside of the coach seat. "City of Joy, I always say."

He even let down both windows, so that the inside of the coach smelled of people in the streets and not only of combustion.

They drove straight to the Opera House. Had not Lexi so directed almost immediately he had ingathered Elena? The building had a stone facade in a scholarly classical manner, but was smaller than Elena had expected, or had provided for in her model. A monk was preaching Repentance on the other side of the square in a pulpit improvised from carbine boxes. All the time Elena could hear his words through the open window.

But Lexi proclaimed too: "Alight, enter, and conquer," he cried out when the carriage had come to a standstill.

"Aren't you coming too?" gasped Elena, too appalled to think.

"I am the administration and the finance, and it is not for administration and finance to break rudely in upon parturition and interpretation."

The dogs were silently clustering round the coach in their usual way, despite all the urban uproar, and the men on the box were beginning to thwack one another, in sport or otherwise.

"I can't go in alone," gasped Elena, too scared to breathe, let alone to move her legs, or even her arms.

"It was what you intended, mademoiselle."

Elena thought about that for half a minute at least.

"So it was," she then said, and began to gather herself together, even though she was shaking as Lexi had shaken after he had suddenly kissed her.

"You are under a spell," Lexi reminded her.

Elena nodded.

Then she turned to Lexi. The men on the box were now punching rather than thwacking. For a moment they reminded Elena of her brothers. Elena straightened her dress.

"Thank you, Lexi. Without you, I should have had many troubles." She believed it was a line from Pushkin, or, if not, then from someone else.

"Without you, mademoiselle, I should have had for company only my ancestors, my serfs, and my mission." Elena almost giggled at his high, thin voice.

"We shall meet at the opera."

Elena was drawing on her different and better gloves.

"I enter only at crisis, mademoiselle."

"Then—"

Shaken once more, Elena stopped pulling for a second or two.

"I am in the hands of my mission; you of your Muse."

"What *is* your mission, Lexi?" After all, it was the first she had heard of it; at least in so many words.

"To free Russia."

In Lexi's case, it really did seem unlikely, despite what he had said to her when the dragoons were blocking the road. But Elena had learned by now that the most surprising men commonly said something of the kind, and that it was never worth pestering or arguing.

Elena, sensible always, dismounted from the carriage, therefore, with her few small objects. Birs and Fors were in no position to offer any help. In the square before the Opera House, it was not too hot, as in the coach, or too cold, as in the abodes of the Countess and the Baron; it was perfect.

"Thank you, Lexi." And Elena curtsied most beautifully.

She would of course be doing that more and more. How invaluable had been all her practice with Tatiana and the others!

There was even a strip of colored carpet or drugget all the way up from the teeming gutter into the heart of the structure, or at least into the interior. The strip was worn in places, especially at the edges, and Elena realized that it was probably stretched for a very grand personage who had attended or was about to attend; but she preferred to believe that it was the spell rising to its first climax.

Lexi was waving *adieux* from the open window. The dogs seemed more numerous than ever, and also, Elena had to admit, more unearthly. Birs was leaning one way on the box, Fors the other way. The monk had begun to denounce her as a brand for the burning. Doubtless all of her kind were included, but his finger was pointing at her personally, as she was well aware. His present congregation of strollers and visionaries was small, his language confused and chiliastic.

Nothing remained but for Elena to enter the Opera House and her destiny.

The first person she met was Irash himself. He was dressed in what she took to be working costume.

"You are rather late," he cried, springing about as he looked up at the big gilt clock in the elaborate foyer. Elena saw at a glance that the clock was wrong.

"We were delayed on the road by dragoons," explained Elena.

"We? Is there anyone else?"

"I was given a lift by someone you know. The Patron of the Opera, Prince Popelevski."

"We seldom see the Prince. He is often a thousand versts away. He is a Freemason."

"I thought so," said Elena, a little smugly.

"If the Tsar but knew!" cried Irash, casting his eyes up to the ceiling, painted with martial gods and half-martial goddesses.

Elena was not sure in what tone Irash had spoken. So she simply said, "The Tsar cannot know everything." She had noticed that it was always an acceptable response.

"To work!" cried Irash, as if everything else was a waste of time.

Elena noticed also that he was no longer addressing her as Mademoiselle. She resigned herself to being clay in his hands.

"I suppose I ought to start with exercises and things?" The book had been far from a working manual.

"You are too late for that," cried Irash, leaping an inch or so in the air, possibly with impatience.

"Then I ought to rehearse?"

"Too late," cried Irash, leaping again.

"Then what am I to do?"

"Come upon the stage and meditate." Though Elena had never before meditated, the idea in other respects exceeded her wildest dreams. She tried to disclose no excitement. By now she was all but trained in reserve, in showing and feeling nothing, or as little as possible.

She and Irash were alone in the great void. The curtain was down, and there was only a single gaslight, high as a fixed star. Irash stood silent, as at a previous critical moment in their life together. Elena meditated on what to ask or say.

"Where is the scenery?" she asked at length.

"You had no time to paint scenery."

"No," said Elena. "I had to leave at once."

"We can do without scenery," said Irash. "Soon most people will do without it."

"Oh, I do hope not," cried Elena. "It was simply that I had not time."

"Fortunately, you completed your dress."

"Yes," said Elena doubtfully. She was far from sure of her workmanship. "But is it the right red?"

"The audience will decide that."

Elena shuddered slightly. But at that moment the risk did not seem very great. Elena darted to the place where the curtain parted in the middle and tugged a corner of its outer surface into the faint gaslight.

"Incredible!" she cried. The curtain was blue, and somewhat crumpled, and the bottom of it was spangled with silver.

Irash tripped across the stage and seized her arm.

"You must try on your dress," he cried. "You may have grown stouter or slimmer on the journey."

"Slimmer, I think," said Elena, a matter, surely, of importance to a dancer.

They tore along black and dusty passages; raced up steep, broken, and endless stairs. They reached an area under the roof. It was lighted by gas flames in odd but meaningful positions. It was tawdry with fabrics. It was very hot from the heaped stove spluttering in one corner beneath the low ceiling.

"This is Grandma Gort," said Irash, waving his arms. "This is Elena Andreievna Timorasieva."

Grandma Gort was all in indigo, with sparse white hair, and a lined face, greened by the gaslight.

"Here I must leave you," said Irash. "I have the opera to interpret as well as the ballet to create."

Without a single word, Grandma Gort began to undress Elena. Elena never thought to object because, as soon as she had entered the room, she had seen the red dress. It glowed, not as if the stovelight were reflected in her Mother's eyes, but as if it had been a live and breeding ruby.

In an unbelievably short time Elena was wearing the dress, and Grandma Gort was making good the errors, pulling and tightening, thrusting in long pins everywhere, several of which entered Elena also. Each time Elena gasped, but she realized that the life of the theater was often much harder than ordinary people fancied. The book had left her in no doubt of that.

Everything in the world seemed to require sacrifice, Elena thought in the middle of the pushing and pulling. All the more reason, perhaps, for not going in for it unnecessarily. She would endure like an Aztec maiden on the altar. Her distant cousin, Admiral Marek Vassilievitch Molotov, had played his part in digging some of them up during the days of the Mexican Empire. She noticed that a thin dark girl had set down her sewing and emerged from the many shadows.

With a final sharp twist to the bodice Grandma Gort was finished and signaled that Elena was to disrobe. Elena made to scramble into her tunic and skirt, far too hot for life in a theater costume room. But Grandma Gort signaled for her to desist. Elena walked over to the stove and waited. She wondered if Grandma Gort was dumb, like their postman at home, who had been committed for opening all the letters, including the most passionate and intimate love letters.

Grandma Gort might speak little or not at all, but now she was doing six other things at once: drawing in and letting out; lengthening and shortening; tacking and splicing. Needles gashed, scissors slashed. Pins flashed like dragonflies.

Elena glanced at the other waiting girl, and smiled slightly. Then—

"Asmara!" she cried.

It was impossible but true, as at the moment were so many things.

Asmara smiled slightly too, but instantly raised her right forefinger and laid it vertically across her lips. Asmara, though still very thin, appeared to be coughing her life out no more.

Elena, smiling still, tiptoed across the room and extricated a bonbon from the pocket of her gray tunic. After her journey, it was the last one left. She held it out to Asmara, indicating in dumb show that it might have suffered on the way and from the heat of the costume room. Still smiling, Asmara accepted it, indicating in dumb show that these dilapidations mattered not at all, but that she was sorry about the lack of a bonbon for Elena.

Soon the alterations to the red dress were completed and now it was adhering to Elena like a dream. The various excellent semiprofessional dressmakers in her small town could not, between them, have achieved in years what Grandma Gort had achieved in what seemed like minutes. But of course the original design had still been Elena's and unaided even by a watercolor drawing.

Asmara indicated in dumb show that Elena should descend to be inspected by Irash. Asmara went first, as Elena could not yet remember the way. Previously, Asmara could never have descended all those dark and broken and endless stairs, let alone climbed up them again.

"Asmara," said Elena, "I *am* so glad."

Asmara did not stop to look back at her, because of the steps, but Elena knew that she was still smiling.

When they reached the stage, Asmara turned and spoke in her soft voice. "Thank you, Elena Andreievna."

"But what happened?" gasped Elena, from within her tight bodice.

"I am well again," was the only explanation Asmara had time to offer before Irash advanced, and stretched out his hand. Elena noticed that it was very dark in color and very hairy.

"Timorasieva!" he said reverently. "The name is perfect."

Elena had never deemed it to be anything but a quite usual name, nor had Tatiana ever differed from this. Now her name began to crackle and sparkle round its edges.

Irash's eyes were taking in every detail at once.

"Do you like my dress?" inquired Elena, twirling a bit, as if truly still with Tatiana.

"It has been always in the mind of time," said Irash. Elena knew she had designed the dress herself, but she saw that both things could be true at the same moment.

There was a pause while Irash continued to gaze at her.

"Shall I go back and take it off?" asked Elena in the end.

"No, the audience is assembling."

Elena realized that in a way it was just as well because Asmara had slipped away, her guide through the ascending labyrinth.

Elena had been aware of the noises on the other side of the curtain. They reminded her of the first sounds at the weekly cattle and horse market, though every time it was far, far noisier when she had woken up properly. One of the girls in the book had spoken of audiences as cattle, but that had been when the girl was in a bad temper.

"I stay here until I dance?" inquired Elena. On the stage it was none too warm, and she was wearing fewer clothes, but exertion would no doubt compensate. The book had spoken of *coryphées* frequently perspiring, even though not of the ballerina doing so.

"You do," said Irash, once more the disciplinarian. He walked towards her. "Watch." With his left hand, he made a curving, complex gesture in the air quite slowly. To Elena it was like scooping a beautifully proportioned segment from a big round moon. Certainly, it was fascinating.

Then Irash touched her right cheek with his pointed lips. It was far from Lexi's peculiarly fervid embrace, at the recollection of which Elena still had to draw upon all her reserves.

"See that no one notices anyone else," said Irash.

"But isn't the ballet in the middle of an opera?" The book conveyed that all ballets were.

"It is," said Irash. He pointed with his brown finger. "There is a room through there with a golden divan. Lie down and rest. You will hear sounds from time to time, and in the end the boy will come to you."

"Which boy?" asked Elena.

"The black boy. He is descended from the Imperial pages."

Fortunately there was a golden fleece or coverlet, as well as a golden divan, or Elena's legs would have frozen, which she knew would have been all wrong. The golden divan was a stage divan, not really meant to be comfortable. For regular use Elena would have preferred the less ornate object in her Father's room. So many people seemed to speak of gold in this inexact way.

However, Elena had no wish to rest, even though she knew that everyone did, and that it was what one was supposed to do. As she lay there, thoughts were beginning to race about within her, and manifold sensations. It was as if her brain were being penetrated by a dozen swords, entering from all directions at once. It was at least as much a torment as a revelation.

The idea that had begun to stir within her when Lexi had spoken of her needing no tuition if in the hands of Irash now linked with a dream she often had. It was not one of those dreams that happen again and again and always terminate at the same tantalization. Mikhail's Aunt Tosha often said she had a dream like that, though she never went into detail, but merely looked momentarily ethereal, churning up the bonbon mixture the while. With Elena the experience was a dream situation that took a different form almost each time, or so it seemed.

Sometimes she was an orator, called upon to rouse an assembly of women, stretching to the horizon, and beyond it.

Sometimes she was a diva, for whom all the women in the enormous hall were waiting in unbelievable silence.

Sometimes she was a cook, with a hundred or more distinguished ladies waiting, mostly in gala dress.

Sometimes she was a divine healer, and female victims of the plague, the palsy, and of paroxysms clustered thickly round the dais, raising clasped hands.

Sometimes even she was a young man in gorgeous uniform, at whose word armies would live or die—certainly one army, ranged in ranks before and around her at that moment.

A common factor was that Elena had no rhetoric; could not sing with power or in tune (Mikhail had confirmed that); was soon bored when trying to follow a recipe; felt people were going to die, herself included, when they were in the least indisposed; and, as has been seen, resisted all politics, let alone strategy, tactics, supply, and heroic sacrifice.

On certain occasions, the form of the experience subtly differed, though Elena felt that really it was still the same experience, the same dream.

Thus: while she had seen as many pictures of the Tsar as everyone else, she sometimes dreamed that she was one of a throng assembled to acclaim him; and that when the Tsar appeared, he was a small man, clean-shaven, myopic, and not at all handsome or well-dressed. In the dream she always knew perfectly well that this could not possibly be the Tsar, but she simultaneously realized that as everyone said it was, she must be mistaken. Somehow she had at that moment learned what the Tsar really looked like, and yet she knew that she had not. The whole experience was doubtless mixed up with the disappointment she had often felt at meeting people who had been frequently described and talked about, but very much more than that was involved. Things were involved that she could not trace at all.

At least once she had been taken in a dream to see a performance by the great actress, Rachel, and Rachel had proved to be enormously tall, and blond, and not at all Jewish: more like an ordinary peasant woman. "That can't be Rachel," she had actually whispered to her Father. "Of course it is Rachel," her Father had whispered back in his stop-talking intonation. Once again: it was and it was not.

Rest, in fact, was absurd. In the small room was a tall looking glass, with the usual gilt edges. Elena sprang up, and began to examine her reflection. Was she the same person, especially in this strange dress which she had designed and made, and yet had not designed and made?

Elena realized that her very lack of any musical gift necessitated the most instant proficiency at the dance.

Elena wished that Bábaba had not abstracted her ananas, meaning nothing but the best.

Into this tall glass, the star should gaze and beseech.

Elena had heard nothing at all of any opera. She heard only voices praising and cautioning.

Elena saw by reflection that the black boy was in the room. He wore a silver suit as if he were his own ancestor. Elena crossed herself. She followed the black boy.

There, at the side of the stage by which the ballerina entered to a storm of applause, stood Irash, elegantly dressed now, and making signs in the air, though not the sign of the cross.

And there, Elena saw, were the *coryphées,* ranged in the order of the moon's last quarter. They were dressed simply and identically; perhaps, Elena fully realized, because no one had bothered enough about them. To Elena, they seemed every bit as wooden as in the box. It was to be hoped that Irash would prove to have done something for them, where she had not.

Elena stood quite still for a second. Then she advanced upon the stage, and there was a storm of applause, exactly as promised.

Elena curtsied carefully, while everybody clapped and yelled. She saw that even the Military Governor was present in his box, with a gypsy woman. Down below, the conductor indicated a thump to his crew. Elena rose upon her points, and lifted both arms into the same quarter of the moon.

It was not the dream. Realizing that, Elena was inspired by an overwhelming wave of happiness.

Baron de la Touque would guard and guide her, if necessary. But everyone present would guard and guide her also. Everyone. Everyone.

Irash was on his knees again, but both knees on this occasion—and at the side of the stage.

"Incomparable. Perfection. Divinity."

Words like that streamed from him; Elena remembered that ballerinas can marry only their business managers. Embarrassingly, she had little wish to marry Irash. She had no idea why not. At that age, one seldom asks. A few yards away the tornado of applause was still raging. Elena could never have survived such a scene had it not been for her book and her model. The police might have to be sent for yet, perhaps the Cossacks.

Soon Elena was in a quite different room, filled with costumes and shoes and accessories and flowers; all without number, all presumably hers. There were several middle-aged women in grimy wrappers—presumably hers also. It was as hot as in the costume room, if not hotter. That might have been partly on account of the crowd which was all the time pouring through the one door, emitting heat and compliments; some of the compliments many-faceted, many-edged, multipurposed. Refreshments were being shuffled about also. Elena wondered how much champagne she would have to drink. So far she had never exceeded two small glasses, much smaller than these; and French champagne she had never yet attempted, though only through lack of opportunity.

"Where is Asmara?" Elena called out as best she could. After all, Elena was supposed to be the cause of all this turmoil, though she was wise enough to speculate upon what could be happening to the opera people meanwhile. She knew that they probably had horses and elephants to look after as well as themselves. Perhaps they were preoccupied.

Disappointingly, the throng merely giggled at Elena's inquiry. She realized that the Military Governor had not yet entered. Doubtless there would be welcome silence when he did. Irash would be escorting him. Then would be the time when her lightest request would be granted. Elena hoped she would not faint before the moment came.

The people in the room were beginning to argue about where Elena had better spend the night. The scene corresponded to the description in the book, though the details were different. Many of the people adhered for only a few seconds to any single subject. It would not have been *bon ton* to go beyond that.

"Please give me a glass of water," said Elena to one of the women in wrappers. Instantly it was in her hand, as always in Russia, whether bond or free, as Lexi might have described the alternatives. Elena sank upon a gold-painted chair in order to drink it. The chair seemed so weak that Elena wondered about the other stars who had sat on it: stars of opera, perhaps. The people in the room, though still increasing in number, would soon be losing interest in her altogether, unless something conclusive happened. She realized that it was only to be expected.

But a skinny woman in a dress which was the same

dull brown from chin to ankle had clutched hold of both Elena's arms, nearly knocking over the glass.

"She is mine."

A tiny moment of less din could have been detected by keen ears. Elena fancied there were even some hints of rivalry. But there are always hints of rivalry, and by no means least when an audience is eating from one's hand, like the horses and elephants.

"The star always goes with me. It is the tradition."

It was not what Elena wanted to do at all, but the reference to tradition made her hesitate. Moreover, she fully realized that it was necessary for her to spend the night somewhere, and not, for choice, among the street mountebanks or with the chanting nuns. Elena took another sip of water.

Then the woman in the brown dress was lifting her up and dragging her, face to face, through the preoccupied multitude. Elena, so vague about age, thought she might be little more than forty, though her hair was quite gray. Elena had perceived that it is childish to think people older than they are.

"It is less than an hour away," hissed the woman into Elena's face. She hissed because she had little spare breath amid her exertions. She had the eyes of an eagle. Several times, Elena had seen eagles only inches away.

"I must get my real clothes," hissed Elena, closely squeezed.

"You will need no clothes."

"I may be cold," hissed Elena, managing to be practical even in such terrible heat.

"I have furs," hissed the woman. Again, it might have been an eagle speaking to her.

Now they were through the one door, and many people in the room were waving elaborate *adieux,* throwing kisses and flowers and peppermints, or shouting "Come again." The woman herself was preventing any of them from emerging.

In the passage, strong and dark as in a prison, it was not merely chilly always but draughty now. Probably the heat in various places dragged cold air from other places; especially at midnight, which Elena realized that of course it now must be. The crowd in the room might feel no wish to emerge.

A slender figure advanced towards Elena, carrying a vast fur cloak. Elena supposed the figure was a young man, because of the costume, and the burden, but as soon as the figure spoke, Elena knew otherwise.

"I am Tatiana's distant cousin, Anna Ismailova Gorsakova. I am here to rescue you." As the figure spoke, she dropped the heavy furs over Elena's head and shoulder, almost bringing her to the ground with the enormous weight.

"Do I need rescue?" asked Elena, struggling upwards.

"Yes. But I am in disguise and can say no more now."

The woman in the brown dress was striding towards

them. There were still one or two people interested enough to watch the scene from the door, each with a glass in one hand and a sausage or chop in the other.

"Yes, thank you. But I still ought to get my real clothes."

"There is no time," said the woman in an offhand way. "Vassily has gone to call the carriage. The bed will be heated when the word is given."

Elena supposed that Vassily was Anna Ismailova Gorsakova. Certainly the latter, after her warning, had instantly disappeared.

The woman pushed Elena into the street.

Outside was a very large carriage, much larger than Lexi's. There were lighted lamps and candles at every corner, without and within. This time a footman in a white wig stood at the carriage door, though Elena could not but wonder whether it was not really a footwoman. The person was very slender and wore the longest possible topcoat. The street was otherwise deserted, except for the many inebriates, and a few first wolves.

The interior of the carriage was like a beautiful drawing room or boudoir: black silk, streaked with gold; a black carpet, enriched with golden asps; small black candles in small golden candelabra; golden ovals containing small likenesses of ballerinas in black, and often with black chaplets. Squatting in a corner of the floor was Anna Ismailova, or Vassily, as the case might be.

The footman shut the door and disappeared some-where. The carriage was in motion; but such motion! It was the second carriage in which Elena had been a guest in one day, but the difference between the two when it came to motion could hardly have been greater. So quiet was the passage that Elena could hear the howling of stray dogs as they passed. Peering through the window, she could see the eyes of stray cats emitting uncertain flashes.

In her own time, the woman in the brown dress spoke again. "When do you dance next?"

"I don't know," said Elena.

"You have much to learn," the woman commented.

"Are you sure?" asked Elena, who would very much have liked to know.

"The greatest dancers in the world have passed the portals of my manor."

Elena shifted herself within the furs. "You are not the Countess Totin?"

"How dare you?"

At that moment, Anna Ismailova caught Elena's eye.

"I'm very sorry," said Elena hastily.

"You may call me Angel."

"I could not be so familiar."

"It is my wish that you are familiar."

Fearful that the woman might kiss her, as Lexi had done, Elena simply said "I shall try," managing to make the words sound almost eager.

However, no further demand was made, and almost no more was said at all as they glided through the night. It was as if something lay ahead which would speak for itself. The woman was allowing the yellow lids slowly to sink across the pale-brown eye slits. Elena could not succeed in again enlisting a glance from Anna Ismailova, who appeared to be deeply involved in thoughts of her own. Elena realized that they might even be plans. More and more Elena wondered what she herself was doing in such an uncertain situation. At once she perceived the answer: it was, as so often in life (and especially of late), that no alternative had offered. It was not as if she had been Gregori or Boris. She could but speculate what they would have done.

Elena stared out gloomily at the night birds sweeping and swooping round the carriage: mainly ravens and owls, respectively croaking and hooting. Both were said to be such wise and prophetic birds, if only one could understand what they had to say, as Bábaba could, from time to time. In the end, Elena suspected that Anna Ismailova was keeping out of contact deliberately. If the woman in brown had only started to snore like other people, Elena would have ventured upon a whisper. But the woman was probably not asleep at all. Elena knew that eagles close their eyes but never sleep. That was why eagles were in such demand as national symbols, especially those with two heads.

There were at least half a dozen footmen with white wigs to help Elena out of the carriage and into the manor.

Anna Ismailova followed silently but closely. The woman in brown, regardless of the autumnal chill, was throwing out orders in all directions. Elena would have been too polite to hang back in order to overhear what the orders were, even had the attendant footmen not made it impossible. Making the best of things, she strode across the big hall to the blazing fire. It stood in the center, augmenting the four stoves, one in each corner. The smoke was drawn upwards by a fan in the ceiling above. One could hear the servants who were turning the system of screws. Logs were burning, five or six feet long. Elena threw off her heavy fur cloak, and two of the footmen bore it away between them. Two other footmen stood with logs in their arms, lest the blaze diminish for a second. The strong light enabled Elena to examine these footmen more closely. Her decision was that they were less like either men or women and more like either monkeys or apes. She had never before seen body servants like them. And now she was simply surrounded.

Anna Ismailova was standing beside Elena, looking like a drawing in *The Clubman*. As a former sportsman her Father still subscribed to that paper, and sometimes the copies arrived. Elena derived many of her dreams from the back numbers her Father had cast away. Anna Ismailova had just the look she knew so well, of inborn indifference to everything. As well as blazing, the great fire was crackling and roaring, so that Elena dared to attempt a *sotto voce* inquiry.

"What do I have to be rescued from?"

Elena had already made a hundred guesses without one hint from the ravens and owls.

Anna Ismailova replied in exactly what Elena had always supposed the correct *Clubman* tone, though perhaps a little more from the corner of the mouth. "In the end, your hostess consumes her guests. You had better know now."

If it had not been for the bonfire, Elena would have paled like a pearl.

A subdued cry came from her: "She's a bird of prey! I thought that at once."

"I shall rescue you. I am in disguise and can say no more."

"But, Anna Ismailova, you said that before. Please say something else." Elena just stopped herself from extending a hand before the gaze of the simian footman, of whom there were at least four more in the hall, one in each corner, like the stoves. Who knew how many there were in all? How many wigs could be needed?

"Silence, Elena Andreievna. There is danger in speech."

And, indeed, the woman in the brown dress was at that moment entering the hall, bringing many more footmen with her. Glancing at them, Elena remembered that monkeys do not look alike to other monkeys, but only to humans.

"Begin to heat the bed," the woman called out harshly.

Footmen sped away in all directions, leaving perhaps only half a dozen in addition to the six fixed in their positions.

Could there only be one bed? Elena wondered. She began to gasp and shiver at the same moment. Anna Ismailova remained impassive as a *billiardiste*.

"Before sleep we must eat and drink, and hold a short conversation," pronounced the woman in brown.

Some of the footmen began to draw back part of the wall. Elena saw that up some steps was a table littered with flowers, some in season, some out, and, among the flowers, foodstuffs that Elena had never so much as imagined. The plates were fully enameled in gold, each with a cockatrice in the middle. Wine was in limpid flasks, tea in translucent samovars. The line of footmen on the other side of the table stretched from wall to wall.

Elena wondered what had become of the bouquets which had been piled high around her and cast down upon her and thrown skillfully up at her during the tornado of applause. The book had said that the ballerina normally bestowed her flowers upon her maids and dressers. Elena visualized the women in grimy wrappers unpicking the bouquets: one orchid for you, one orchid for Vera Nikolaevna, one orchid for little me. And so on.

As Elena began to ascend the steps, like Amédée in "La Belle Ensorceleuse," the two footmen at the fire cast in their big logs with a crash and a fountain of sparks. They stooped, and immediately were bearing new logs, like coats of arms.

Other footmen enclosed Elena in a cloak of unnumbered feathers, all bright, all different. Her cousin, Admiral

Marek Vassilievitch Molotov, had brought back fragments of such cloaks from Mexico. In his unfinished book he had spoken of their significance. Elena, who, though required to read the book, had only glanced at it, as it was all in handwriting, could not remember what the significance was, even if she had ever reached that far. It seemed all too possible that the cloaks were worn by sacrificial victims, but then most things in old Mexico were. She glanced in panic at Anna Ismailova, but Anna, *vrai homme du monde,* had started to eat and drink, as if at home everywhere.

Indeed, there proved to be nothing very remarkable about the meal that followed, apart from the gorgeousness of the surroundings, the rarity of the fare, and the elegance of the vintages. Elena, however, had still not attained to French champagne. There was not even Russian champagne: only exquisite, soporific, runic still wines in miraculous decanters. One was left with the aroma of old and magical raisins. Anna Ismailova was selecting and rejecting with wholly unobtrusive aplomb, and Elena noted that the woman in brown appeared to be picking and pecking much like other women Elena had known of the same apparent age, such as certain so-called aunts, who were really something else.

That amount of wine acted upon Elena like a tonic, but she took particular care not to drink much too much.

The meal ended in bananas. Trotting footmen brought in a whole tree, which had just been slashed down. Probably it had been growing in some outlying conservatory. It cannot be said that all the bananas were eaten by the little group.

"And now for coffee and conversation in the Parrot Room," announced the woman in brown. The mention of parrots made Elena realize that the brown dress was exactly like a bird's working plumage.

Elena had naturally supposed the Parrot Room to be a matter of the wallpaper, perhaps painted in China by tender girls with tiny feet; but, in fact, the walls proved to be covered with a simple Pompeian damask (Mademoiselle Olivier-Page had spoken of Pompeii, and displayed a man's silk handkerchief in that particular red), the parrots to be singing and shouting in cages and from perches. In fact, conversation might well prove unnecessary.

"Mind your nose and both ears," Anna Ismailova managed to enjoin, as she strolled languidly onward. Elena shrank into herself. But perhaps her feathery cloak would acclimatize her.

The coffee table stood in the middle of the room, almost certainly out of pecking distance. Elena essayed a little rush to reach it. She had read in her book of a quick succession of pattering steps. It conveyed virginity and innocence and girlishness, and was said to be charming.

Elena collapsed into a carved teak chair with a cushion like an orange, but very nearly jumped up again. She had realized that there were no footmen in the room. Only parrots, macaws, cockatoos.

She remembered the words of Mikhail's song, the very

last song she had heard him sing. Homesickness overwhelmed her for a moment.

Anna Ismailova was reclining on a heap of rugs, like a university student, needing only the little cap, the little beard, the little roulette pistol. With her own hand the woman in brown was pouring the blackest possible coffee into crystal glasses, like skulls.

"Shall we talk about shooting?" asked the woman, as if it mattered little what the subject might be. Her seat was made of mammoth tusks. The honey skin of a wild horse was draped over it. It was like Tamerlane's throne.

"I don't know about shooting," replied Elena, with justified sulkiness.

"Can you ride?"

"Not very well."

"Travel, then. Where have you been?"

"Nowhere," said Elena truthfully.

"I see that you will never be content unless we talk about your own career. I must tell you that you lack edge. You are only at the start. You lack sharpness. You need to be honed like a razor."

"Do you think so?" Elena had often watched Stefan Triforovitch honing for her Father. He did it in the little yard where the cows used to be, and Silke turned the wheel. She had always wondered how soon the slender steel would be completely honed away.

"I can make you glint and flash. Only then will you

[99]

dominate. I have finished off many of the greatest dancers in the world."

The woman put down her glass, rose to her feet, and began to demonstrate what she meant, as so many people do when the art of the dance is the subject. After forty or fifty seconds of inconclusive oscillation, she made a sudden battering plunge, as if to establish her point in one instant. To Elena it was as if a hawk had stooped upon a burrowing mole, though of course a brown hawk.

"That is what it is like to be finished," said the woman. Her voice grated ferally.

The woman then walked slowly back to her throne of old ivory. Her eyes were half-closed and her expression replete. Elena noticed that Anna Ismailova was now sitting up, with her feet upon the onyx floor. She was wearing the most exquisite shoes.

Seated once more, the woman was entirely as usual. "Being a ballerina is more than just a matter of what one looks like," she said in her nonchalant way.

"Yes, I know," said Elena earnestly. The very same remark had been uttered by someone or other in her book. Elena was beginning to understand that the number of sentiments that can be put into words is definite and limited. If she had managed to read one book, she had probably read all of them.

"Vassily," said the woman. "Pour us all some more coffee."

It was as if she was tired of conversation. Indeed, she gave a curious matter-of-fact yawn, just as if she had been a man among men, or a raptor among raptors.

All the while the plumed spirits of the jungle were of course bawling their immodesties and screeching assorted staves from *"Una voce poco fa."* Elena realized that one bird was simply repeating "Fly. Fly. Fly." She could not help but turn to look. It was a plain and rather small African parrot in dark gray, with only a trace of pink tail feather. Her Father had once said it was the species that "talked best," as he put it. He knew one that had prophesied every death and illness for more than a century.

"They were all once human," said the woman, as if it hardly mattered one way or the other.

"They have the most beautiful colors," said Elena politely, for some reason casting off her own feathered cloak at just that moment. After her long day, she too yawned, but in moderation, and at least with an attempt at pretending it was a show of interest.

"They are captive souls," continued the woman.

As Elena was by now out of her depth, it was as well that Anna Ismailova spoke for her. It was almost the first time Anna Ismailova had entered the general conversation.

"They are ventriloquists' dolls," said Anna Ismailova.

"They are wiser than the ventriloquists," said the woman.

After divers further *causeries* and rallies, touching upon every subject they could think of, the woman in the brown dress most kindly herself showed Elena to her room, and pointed out the right bed, one among many beds, when they had arrived there.

"Be prepared," Anna Ismailova had muttered, instead of the usual "good night." She might have been a youthful Lieutenant General. She did not even kiss Elena, though Elena would have found a kiss reassuring.

Elena wondered what had happened to all the footmen. Doubtless they were insensible up trees, or disposed by hundreds in the rafters, like magpies. Still, one might have expected a few night footmen also, such as those for whom Mozart wrote that delicate music. She was not sure whether to be glad or sorry there were none; and no music either.

Elena was accustomed to sleeping in a large room, but this one would have slept all the officers in Suvorov's Grand Patriotic Army. Elena's inmost thoughts were more and more tinged by military analogies. The woman bent over her, grated out "Tomorrow," and kissed her sharply in the middle of her brow. When she had gone, Elena rubbed the place gently with her pocket handkerchief. A nerve runs upward and downward at that point, and even a kiss can inflame.

Elena saw that there was no icon in the room. She crossed herself.

She began to take off her beautiful red dress. The next question would be how best to approach the heated bed. There was only one lamp, exactly as at home, but this lamp was carved in malachite to resemble a boyar, though Elena did not think the resemblance very close. She could see that portraits of many other boyars hung on the walls, all exactly alike, at least by the glimmer of a single lamp.

At the very far other end of the room, a cupboard suddenly opened. Elena screamed. That anything more could happen was unbearable. It reminded Elena once more of her dreams. In dreams happenings never stop. One never rests or sleeps in a dream, or even embarks on quiet reflection, or upon an hour with the poets.

A man was tiptoeing towards her, as, supposedly, in a nightmare: not a dragoon, as hitherto, but a hussar.

"Stop!" cried the hussar. "No, go on."

Before Elena had time to scream again, the hussar said "Hush!" and Elena perceived that it was Anna Ismailova. She next perceived that the conflicting orders related to whether or not she should continue to undress.

"Which?" Elena inquired in fatigued exasperation. Of course she had drunk goblets full of glutinous wine.

"Come over here," bid Anna Ismailova, pointing into the cupboard. "You must dress like me."

"I am too small!" cried Elena.

"Boys are equal now with men," explained Anna Ismailova. "The Tsar has decreed it."

"But *why*?" expostulated Elena, referring not to the distant Tsar but to the equally demanding Anna Ismailova.

"We have to walk to Smorevsk, that far at least, and we do not wish to be molested by zanies."

"But it's pitch dark!"

"No. It's dawn." And so it was. The lamp looked as if deep in water.

"I can't walk to Smorevsk. I've been dancing."

"We shall stop at a hut."

"*Must* we go now? Is there no other way?"

"It is the only way," said Anna Ismailova.

It was what Elena's Mother had said only a few days ago.

Elena shivered slightly in the late autumnal daybreak. Then she completed the removal of her dress and of whatever else had to be removed, and began slowly to array herself as ordered. These were not garments to which she was accustomed; not since the parties given by the wife and daughters of the Military Governor, to which every small, respectable child in the small town used to go, willingly or otherwise.

"Hurry!" exclaimed Anna Ismailova. "When it is daylight we shall be visible."

The complete garb would no doubt have been exciting as well as precautionary, an unusual conjunction, but, alas, Elena was too weary for excitement.

"How do we get out?"

"There is a ladder."

Elena peered through the window.

"Bring your red dress," said Anna Ismailova. "Stuff it in your sabretache."

"We ought to be taking food."

"God will provide."

The girls crossed themselves.

There was no boundary wall, no moat or deep ditch, no attempt at a botanical garden, no gate.

There were, however, marks in the sodden soil of animals and immense birds. There was also a very faint drizzle, but perhaps that was permanent. All the leaves were yellowy-brown, and all the trunks and branches fungoid. The silence was so intense as to suggest that nature had ceased to take part in things.

The girls had difficulty in finding a track, even though they knew that while they looked they could still be seen from the manor. As to where the track led, the only pointer was a pocket compass of Anna Ismailova's. Soon, in their gray garb, they had disappeared in the mist.

"How do you know all the things you do know?" asked Elena, plodding as best she could.

"I have been a year at the University," replied Anna Ismailova. "For a year I have been a male."

Of course Elena knew that girls and women could not go to the University, or not as students, and she had also heard from Tatiana that some did as Anna Ismailova had done. Elena now understood how Tatiana had been so confident about that.

"But you can't have learned about every manor in Russia?"

"Not through the curriculum. But some manors are more notorious than other manors. Not much happens in our country, you know, by comparison with its size."

"And about every Opera House in Russia?"

"Tatiana wrote to me that you would soon be a ballerina in Smorevsk."

"And you traveled all this way?"

"No, I was passing through, in any case."

Elena thought it best to accept that. She could not but think of a new question almost at every step, but most of them could wait. At the moment sleep was the need.

A peasant and his wife took them in, as Anna Ismailova had promised. Elena had to admit that it could hardly have happened had she and Anna not been accepted as young officers on the usual secret duty. Anna Ismailova flourished their commission engraved on specially treated parchment, though the peasants could not read it.

The girls were given wooden bowls of rye gruel and shredded marshweed before the peasant couple went out on to their plot, where the sturdy sons were working already. Elena supposed that the family could do very little in the way of marketing, either selling or buying. She herself could not finish more than half the meal, but Anna Ismailova did better. One could see the boxes in which the stalwart sons of the house slept, but the parents had offered the girls the use of their own bed in the back room. Here, as in the front room, the light burned before the icon, and here the wooden walls were roughly painted with holy scenes. Elena, with almost no clothes on at all, was asleep within less than two and a half minutes beneath the heavy coverlet common to all. Anna Ismailova too had been through manifold and various exertions of her own. It had to be admitted that when the time came for the peasant couple to retire, the two young soldiers were not merely still abed but still slumbering. In accordance with the obligations of hospitality, the peasant couple bedded down on the main room floor, surrounded by their stertorous offspring, all male.

It was dawn again when Elena again opened her eyes. Could she have slept continuously for more than twenty-one hours? Lying beside her, Anna Ismailova was smiling with sophistication as she read a novel in a pink and green cover from a private library at the University.

Elena started to scratch, and then recollected that it was the very last thing one should do. For example, Anna Ismailova was hardly scratching at all.

"A life for the Tsar!" cried the master of the hut, as the two officers resumed their march. The track might soon be almost a road.

Both saluted, though not convincingly.

Fortunately, it was too late for anyone to criticize.

"*How long* were we in the carriage? Smorevsk cannot be all this way."

"I do not know and at the University we are told never to guess at anything."

However, Anna Ismailova glanced at her compass. Unfortunately, ever since last night, the compass seemed to have become subject to spells of idle spinning. Elena looked sulky, though she could quite see it was not reasonable so to do. She had brought it all on herself by reading books and making a model and lacking alternatives.

They stumped forward in silence for a long time, with little company but partridges, centipedes, and marsh gas.

At last, Elena spoke out.

"I don't think I want to go back to the Opera House."

"No."

"I don't want to go back home either."

"Tatiana has told me."

"There are threats on all sides, Anna Ismailova."

"But now you are better equipped to meet them, Elena Andreievna."

About an hour later, or so it seemed, Elena spoke again.

"We were right to sell the cows. There was no room for them to turn round. Let alone the bull." She spoke as one conscious at the same time of the comic and tragic sides of the former situation.

"Soon there will be no room for human beings to turn round either, Elena Andreievna."

"Anna Ismailova! Are you a revolutionist?"

"Of course not, Elena Andreievna. There is no such thing as a revolution." It was the very voice of the newly educated female, even though educated in disguise.

"I don't think Lexi agrees with you," said Elena.

"Who may Lexi be?"

"I'll tell you, but not now."

"Our country is full of illusion and illusionists," remarked Anna Ismailova, as if she were more than three times the age she actually was.

But Elena was hardly attending. "Look!" she cried, and, as they were quite alone, stopped to point.

"What is it?" asked Anna Ismailova. All the girls in Tatiana's family had weaker eyes than Elena's, who could at any time differentiate a native gnat from a marauding mosquito in midair, which many found impossible.

"It's the Gates of Smorevsk, of course!"

"I can't see anything."

"Well, I can. Don't worry, I know they're open. In fact, they won't shut."

"Are you sure these are the same gates?"

"No, I'm not, Anna Ismailova, but, if not, we can walk round."

"We ought to be thinking of where we're going

afterwards," said Anna Ismailova, still very much the product of a higher education.

"The Opera House frightens me now. It was like a dream. Anyway, I've done it once. Where do *you* want to go, Anna Ismailova?"

"I'm on a pilgrimage, Elena Andreievna."

"What, to the Holy Black Icon?"

"To nowhere specific. Say to life itself and to the heart of truth." Before Elena's eyes, Anna Ismailova was changing from man of the world into Elena was not sure what. Anna's smile gave little clue, either.

"I'm too young to understand," said Elena, smiling a little herself.

"I feel that I have seen, heard, and known all that there is," cried out Anna, pressing her gauntlets to her eyes.

"I think that may be quite easy to do," said Elena. "Please don't cry, Anna Ismailova. Perhaps you shouldn't have gone to University."

"I had to take experience to the limit, Elena Andreievna. My Father died from frostbite showing our flag in Spitzbergen. My Mother died at a scientific conference."

"I am so sorry," said Elena, putting her arm round Anna's shoulders, which she could not quite reach. "Would you like to sit down? We can listen to the bells from the thousand churches."

It was easier to embrace Anna when they were seated

side by side on a horizontal stone inscribed "Smorevsk 1 Verst" with an arrow, but no arrow pointing in the other direction, and no inscription.

"Listen!" said Elena. "I'm sure you'll feel better." And, suddenly, as on a previous occasion, the sun began to shine quite brilliantly.

"You have stronger eyes than me, Elena Andreievna, and you may have stronger ears also. I have listened to so much."

"Bábaba always says that my ears are far too big."

Be that as it might, Elena now clearly realized that she could hear something coming towards them and from the direction they had come themselves. She sprang to her feet. Yes, yes: she could see creatures and a small coach lumbering in the midst of them.

"Stand up, Anna Ismailova. Do you see all those dogs?"

"No," said Anna Ismailova. "I see only a tumbril of some kind. I see nothing else. I told you."

Elena swiftly changed the subject. "It's Lexi. That's his carriage. Now you'll meet him, and I shan't have to explain anything."

Lexi simply took it for granted that they would want to return to Elena's small town, and there seemed little point in arguing. He knew all about Elena's enormous success two nights before. He quite understood that now she needed a rest, especially as she was still so young: indeed, he did not wait for Elena to say so, but took the initiative in saying so himself, and without mentioning the matter of age. From at least one of his remarks it seemed that he might even know about the peril from which Elena had been rescued. Certainly he expressed no surprise at the way the two girls were dressed. "It is charming, charming," he said. "Delightful, delightful. It will be convenable if we meet the brigands. They are infesting all the roads."

"What's happened to the dragoons?" asked Elena.

"No one knows. Perhaps the brigands have killed them all. Perhaps they have joined the brigands."

Elena would normally have inquired, as people always did, whether they themselves would be safe on the road, but it seemed absurd when she was a hussar, and her rescuer also.

Lexi said he had a little business in Smorevsk, with which it would be unnecessary for the two girls to be involved, but that he would return for them in an hour or two. He gave them a cold baked ptarmigan and a bag of sugared almonds and a small bottle of spirit made from grass seeds. He told them to fear nothing.

Thus reinforced, they spent the noonday hours spinning dreams like cobwebs, and dodging demands like nets.

When they were on their way again, Elena asked whether it might not be far more interesting for them all to stay not with the Baron and the old Countess but somewhere else. Lexi explained that there *was* nowhere else.

Inevitably, the Baron supposed the two girls to be men and wanted them, after the meal, to tourney with selected servants: successively at fist fighting, Russian wrestling, and pikestaff; in that order, he suggested. He remarked that an award of any kind to the winner would, in the circumstances, be a *bêtise,* as his two guests would understand. The girls claimed long overdue dispatches, and locked and barred and wedged themselves in so that they could compile them with exemplary care.

Lexi kept the Baron so occupied thereafter that not a sound was heard all night from the landing. Elena said not one word to Anna about the Baron's evil-looking, shaggy dogs. When it came to dogs, people's vision differed, as well as the power of their eyes.

The old Countess, seeing the two girls through the bars, calmed down to some extent, and proceeded to spend the entire evening and much of the night talking about experiences at the Court of Tsar Paul, who had been as mad as she now was. It seemed incredible to Elena that the Countess could be so old, but it would hardly have been polite to ask, and, anyway, the Countess gave no opportunity.

The hours of darkness seemed more secure with Anna by her side than on Elena's previous visit. When Elena raised the matter of the old Countess's age, Anna merely spoke of important researches that were now going on into all such questions, leading to the provisional conclusions that many people lived hidden away for many, many more years than was generally supposed, and that the secret of longevity seemed to lie entirely in eating and drinking nothing but soured goat's milk. Special bacteria then took charge of one. Madness might also, she thought, prove to be a question of special bacteria, though different ones. Meanwhile, the old Countess had talked so much that she had no energy left to scream, chuckle, and rage.

The bright sunshine outside Smorevsk proved to have been the last for that year, and on this third day snow was falling all the time. It might be a race to reach Elena's small town before the road was blocked for months, though it could not be said that the coach was going particularly fast. Birs and Fors were wearing more and more overcoats; several additional hats, woolly and furry; gauntlets like used cannon balls. Elena and Anna wished they had brought their own full winter issue. They had to make do with Lexi's spare rugs, which smelt and were rather infested.

In the end, falling snow was the whole world.

"I shall proceed from the town by sleigh," announced Lexi, as he puffed. In the cold air, the smoke hung in tendrils.

"Or there's the railroad," Elena suggested helpfully.

"Why not wait for the spring?" asked Anna.

"I cannot wait. I am one who is awaited," averred Lexi in his curiously high voice.

"You seem to be awaited here," remarked Anna, controlled and equable, even though the coach had come to a very sudden stop.

"The brigands!" cried Lexi. "Now show your mettle, boys!"

But the brigands seemed to have little idea of ambushing the party. On the contrary, they were clustered in the middle of the highway, chanting and preoccupied. Their garb was wild and their hair was straggling.

"They are penitent," cried Lexi. "They are suffering."

And indeed Elena could see through the falling flakes that many of the brigands were scourging and biting one another while they intoned. The doggy throng completely encircled the group, awaiting orders as always, even though the orders never came.

"What hope is there for Russia but in sacrifice?" inquired Lexi ecstatically.

In the time available Elena could not think of a reply, and Anna did not attempt one. But all three crossed themselves, and, after a further silent pause, Lexi simply called out "Drive on!"

It was as well that he did so because already the wheels would hardly turn. There was also a risk of at least one wheel being wrenched off. Elena knew that it often happened. Or the central trunk of timber might split in the cold. Or everything and everybody might disappear in a crevasse, only to be found after Easter.

They reached the small town: perhaps miraculously; as so much had already been. It was black. It was snowing. It was freezing. They were outside Elena's Father's house.

The two hussars leapt out as if they had been escorting a chef de cabinet. The snow almost reached the tops of their boots.

"Come with us, Lexi," cried Elena. "My Father would be so pleased to greet you."

She knew it was the proper thing to say, but she doubted whether it was true. Judging by what her Father had said before she left, even the wherewithal might be lacking. Everything might be lacking.

But that problem also solved itself.

"No," said Lexi, smiling and puffing. "I must go to Popelevsk."

"Why?" asked Elena.

"I am Patron of the Athenaeum, the Gymnasium, the Propylaeum."

"Does Irash create in those places?"

But Lexi only smiled. "I must find a sleigh," he said and shut the carriage door, but in the most conclusive manner.

"Thank you, Lexi," said Elena, as the snow fell around her.

"We are so grateful," said Anna.

"I must proceed with my mission," cried Lexi through the closed carriage window.

Dressed as they were, and in deep snow, the girls could hardly curtsy, so the carriage simply dragged off. Elena knew very well that in the old days the serfs were often found frozen to their box.

"What *is* his mission?" asked Anna Ismailova, as they stumbled round to the door used by tradesmen, children, and hens.

"To free Russia," replied Elena, trying to prevent her boots being dragged from her legs. They fitted less closely than her own proper boots, as was only to be expected. Alas, her own proper boots might well have gone forever.

"He will not succeed," said Anna Ismailova, quite seriously.

They entered the large back room, in which Elena stalked cherries, combed out cloudberries, stoned damsons, and counted potatoes. Her Father was standing there, wringing his hands. But he looked up at once.

"Why, Gregori! Why, Boris!"

"You forget, Papa, that Boris is not a soldier but a seminarian."

"Why, so I do. It is a time of trouble for all of us. Who then can you be?"

"I am Elena, Papa, and this is Anna Ismailova, the second cousin of Tatiana Yegorova."

"Not second cousin," muttered Anna, accurately but *sotto voce.*

Elena's Father clasped Elena briefly but parentally in his arms and bowed slightly to Anna Ismailova. Then he began to pace up and down the flagstones, lissome still, though less lissome than of yesterday. He wove effortlessly among the broken chairs, half-filled wooden pails, adapted garden tools, and other oddments.

"There are changes, Elena."

"What are they, Papa?"

"Your Mother is crying out constantly."

"But that is not a change, Papa."

"Bábaba has lost all emotion."

"I am sure Bábaba knows why that is, Papa."

"Stefan Triforovitch is sawing up the cowshed. There is nothing else left." In fact, one could hear Stefan Triforovitch doing it as they talked. Elena's Father turned politely to Anna Ismailova. "We no longer keep cows," he said with a sad smile, but pacing ever.

"They yield better in the pastures," confirmed Anna Ismailova, cautiously reassuring her host.

Elena sank down on to one of the chairs and began to sprawl. Sprawling was actually expected of a young officer. Anna Ismailova sat down also. It was difficult for anyone to decide how long the conversation might continue.

"Cook has gone to her daughter. We have no cook now."

"Papa! I never knew Cook had a daughter."

"Of course. And three sons." Elena's Father was rending the veil of reticence from ceiling to floor, as with a heavy cleaver. There might be nothing he could not disclose. He was turning on his heel ever more frequently, often before he reached the actual wall.

"I myself am totally lost. I am disgraced and ruined. I can do nothing. There is nothing I can do."

He was speaking to the air, rather than to his visible auditors. The air smelt like a toolshed. A reply was left to Elena.

"I am sure there is, Papa. Anna Ismailova will advise you. She's just come from University."

Elena's Father turned to Anna. "Thank you, sir. Only Count Wilmarazov-Totin can help me, and he is distraught."

"Why is that, sir?" asked Anna Ismailova politely.

"He shot at his son in a fit of disappointment. Happily the Mother is at the Baie des Anges and knows nothing."

Elena had sat up a little. "Is Rurik dead?"

"No. It's worse than that."

"Then he is laid up in bed?"

"No. It would be no use."

Elena repressed a little scream. All she said was "Who now does the cooking? Remember that we have a guest, Papa."

"Bábaba does what she can."

"We must find a new cook at once, Papa."

"I am undone, I am undone." Elena's Father unclasped his hands from their usual position behind his back, and began to wave them in the air for a few moments. "Not only I, but my wife, my daughter, our servants. One of them has died from grief."

"Oh, Papa," cried out Elena. "Which one?"

"The Prussian, Silke. He died within twenty-four hours."

"No, no." Elena burst into bitter tears. She was not as accustomed to sad news as she had supposed.

"He was a cripple, sir, and not strong," Elena's Father explained to Anna Ismailova.

Elena's face was sunk between her hands. Anna put her arms round Elena's shoulders.

"Elena Andreievna has had many experiences," she said. "Elena has learned at least half of all there is to know."

Elena's Father stopped moving. He stood as still as he had stood when they had entered the room. He smiled bravely, as if he had been a statue: "The son of my client Count Wilmarazov-Totin may yet be able to teach her the other half. I pray for that."

Elena stopped crying.

"How is Asmara, Papa?" she asked, in a new, low, cold voice, which took her completely by surprise.

But her Papa had never heard of Asmara, or at least not by name. He addressed Anna Ismailova.

"You are welcome, sir," he said, with the same brave smile, which had not left his features for a moment. "You are welcome to take up residence in my depleted, denuded, despairing home."

"I am obliged," said Anna Ismailova, once more the man of the world. "I have in mind to disturb you only for a single night."

"*Half the pain* in the world is caused on purpose, the other half by mistake," remarked Anna Ismailova, as they looked about for Bábaba, who had not been found in the kitchen, nor anyone else.

"I shall go back to the ballet, whether I like it or not," said Elena.

"I expect you will like it," said Anna Ismailova, now man of the world and reassuring friend at the same time.

In the end they found Bábaba patching blankets in the mending room, which was big and draughty. Some of the patches were pink, some dark green, some so faded that one could not divine how they had begun.

Bábaba did not even shriek when they entered. Elena's Father had never fully realized who Elena was, but Bábaba knew at the first second, even by the light of a single candle.

"So you've come back," Bábaba said. "Stand away. Don't try to embrace me."

Elena's arms fell to her side. But she could see that Tosha was sitting on the floor, under the icon, and helping—in black, as always, from chin to ankle. Her chestnut hair was drawn back as in the ballet, but for different reasons.

"I am a distant cousin of Tatiana Yegorova," announced Anna, obviating misinformation.

"You could have counted upon ending in a way you didn't expect," said Bábaba, more or less to both of them, it seemed.

"Yes, Bábaba, I know that," said Elena.

"I suppose you're dressed up for the Military Governor's wife's party, but it's not till Christmas, and you're too old anyway."

Bábaba had at least noticed their costume, where Elena's Father probably had not. However, it was the first time, as far as Elena could remember, that anyone had specifically said she was too old for anything. Bábaba had been the first to break all important news since Elena had occupied the cramped cot.

"I had to be rescued," explained Elena, who always told Bábaba everything, or nearly everything. "We're prepared to change now."

"I have nothing to change into," said Anna Ismailova, who was quite the wrong shape for any of Elena's dresses, and the wrong coloring also, being darker than a prune, whereas Elena was fair as an apple blossom.

"I'm so sorry," said Elena.

"I don't mind," said Anna, smiling.

"You're both too old for jokes," said Bábaba calmly, and without ceasing to patch for a single moment.

All the while Tosha's hand had been flitting from one

pocket or another to her mouth. Her legs must have been cold inside her dress, which was not very thick, but now she rose upon them, and approached the young warriors with two *papier mâché* pokes in each of her hands, even though her hands were very small.

"Cinnamon. Nutmeg. Rhubarb. Metheglin."

Elena selected one of each, but Anna accepted only the nutmeg, and that for the sake of former times, even though her own former times had not been passed in this particular house.

All through the evening meal (how else could one define it?), Elena's Father continued to speak of the troubles that had descended upon all of them. Again, Anna Ismailova seemed to be included, perhaps out of courtesy to a guest. Even the foodstuffs were of the kind most readily obtainable, and often of the kind most easily prepared. Do what she could, Elena could not but endure the most detailed recollections of the fare in the house of the woman called Angel. After all, she had consumed so much of it. Had it been only four nights previously?

"Who cooked this, Papa?" enquired Elena, extending her fork, and rudely interrupting her Father's *pensées*, even though they must have been all the more difficult for him to hold on to, in that one by no means descended logically or naturally from another.

Papa broke off, which previously he had seemed unable to do. He began to arrange his posture as if for conventional intercourse. He drew in some new breath.

Elena pressed on. "It can't have been Bábaba, Papa?" She twirled her fork like a dervish.

But all her distracted Father said was, "Eat what is put before you, Elena. Many would find it luxury. Soon there will be nothing."

He could identify Elena more easily now that she was again wearing a mended dress.

He appealed with agonized eyes to Anna Ismailova, the guest in the house.

"I find everything perfectly *de rigueur,* sir," responded Anna gravely.

"You must share my room," said Elena, clutching Anna's arm, "or I shall be frightened." They were standing in pitch darkness at the foot of the staircase. Elena's Father had removed the one lighted lamp and in his study could be heard circling round it like a moth.

Moreover, no particular room had been offered to Anna Ismailova. Bábaba seemed to have relinquished control over everything except the patching and hemming. The house had come to illustrate the theories of the Anarchists. Madame's obsession with hygiene had become quite *passé* and irrelevant.

"I'm not sure that I can rescue you a second time, Elena Andreievna," said Anna, still gravely, in the dark.

"What nonsense!" cried Elena. "Of course you can. Every time."

They stumbled upstairs, hitting things with their feet and hands. Anna was momentarily involved with a device that had no business to be there: it was used by Gregori and Boris for catching kingfishers.

Elena lighted her bedroom lamp, as she often did, from the short, fat candle before the icon, though it was supposed to be an impropriety.

"Now I should like to see the model," said Anna Ismailova.

Elena hesitated for several seconds.

She might have reached another turning point or revelation. But the suggestion had not come as a complete surprise.

She pulled herself together, chilly though the room was. "So should I," she said. "I've never set eyes upon it in the dark."

Elena lighted the way as best she could up the further stairs, much as the black pages lighted the officers to the higher boxes.

Even outside the closed attic door, the two of them could hear the hubbub.

"Anna Ismailova," said Elena in a voice which, though very low, was far now from being cold or new. "Anna Ismailova, it's going to be gorgeous." She did not even seize hold of Anna, but, for a moment, stood proudly, solitarily, with arms upraised, like the arms of the Woman from Samothrace, though when that Woman had been younger.

Then Elena threw back the door, causing a thump that would never have been endured below in the old days, certainly not by Bábaba, let alone by Gregori and Boris, though least of all by Elena's Father as he used to be.

An improvised workroom was full of people seated at different levels upon *fauteuils*. Even from the back, one could see how well dressed they all were: some of the ladies wore *aigrettes,* which they had not removed or abbreviated. At the directions of the Imperial Chamberlain upon such matters these ladies merely laughed delightfully on almost all occasions.

The orchestra was tinkling and rippling delightfully too, and Elena saw at once, even from the rear, that it was Irash who conducted it. There were few limits to that man's capacities: had not Lexi said something of the kind? Elena also saw that seated not in the Imperial Box (which was apparently unoccupied), but in the sinister box opposite, almost equal in dimensions, though of course not quite equal, was Angel, aureoled by her semi-simian footmen, some dangling from the cartouches. Elena knew at once, if only by intuition, that Angel always, always occupied the box opposite the Imperial Box. Elena unobtrusively crossed herself.

The blue curtain must have gone up some time ago because a few of the gentlemen in the audience were breathing heavily; some of them young gentlemen. Perhaps they were among those more interested in the opera than in the ballet, as many are. Nonetheless the *coryphées* looked convincing, hardly at all wooden. At the center of it all the ballerina, in her red dress, spun round and round, without ceasing, upon the unassailable top pinnacle of her sunbeam fame: la Gitana to the life. At first glance, only the scenery was in need of much further thought.

"It's still beautiful, Anna Ismailova," gasped Elena. "It's still beautiful."

"In any case, it's a beautiful theory, Elena Andreievna," said Anna, smiling academically but not unkindly.

And, in the morning, Anna was simply not there. It was as when Frau Barger von Meyrendorff had failed to appear upon her hour, having been whisked out of the house before midnight by Elena's Mamma.

Such was the breakdown and disorder in the establishment that it was Elena's Father himself who announced to Elena at about half-past eleven in the morning that a gentleman wished to see her. He was awaiting her in her Father's study.

"It's not Count Wilmarazov-Totin?" Elena asked at once, before taking one step. She was keeping her voice down, and diligently remustering all her forces. Already she had had to hunt about for her own breakfast. The guinea fowls had either been killed and eaten, or, in most cases, had escaped from the slaughterers and, it was to be hoped, found someone else to look after them.

Elena's Father simply shook his head, with the saddest smile imaginable. Needless to say, he should long ago have been at work and properly in pursuit of the sums properly owing.

"It's not—?" asked Elena with a gulp.

Again her Father shook his head, this time more seriously. Would Elena ever know with any precision what had happened to the entity in both their minds? She hoped not.

She followed her Father into his den. The room looked more downtrodden every time she entered it.

"This is Count Oplotkin," said her Father. A middle-aged gentleman in a long frock coat rose from the Sportsman's Chair. Elena curtsied.

"You know who *he* is?" inquired her Father.

Elena shook her head. His very fair hair would have emitted attractive gleams in the light from the window, if it had been a different time of year.

"I am from St. Petersburg," said the gentleman. "From the Imperial Opera."

"You see!" said Elena's Father, drawing himself together like a jack-in-the-box about to expel itself.

"I have a proposal to make to you, mademoiselle."

"A proposal?" asked Elena doubtfully.

"You must not expect too much."

"Of course not," said Elena, without really thinking, because she was so relieved by the implication of the words as to the type of proposal.

"We should be prepared to consider training you as a character dancer."

"There!" cried Elena's Father, and began to pace elastically up and down, and around all obstacles.

"What is that?" asked Elena. Oddly enough, all three of them were still in one way or another on their feet.

"I must tell you quite plainly that it is not to be a ballerina, mademoiselle."

"Oh!" cried Elena.

"Being a ballerina is more than just a matter of what one looks like."

Elena was unsure whether she ought to bow her head or raise it.

"You are too old to start the training in that direction," said Count Oplotkin primly, but with a gentle smile beneath his trimmed gray moustache.

It was the second time Elena had been debarred as too old. Of course, it was bound to happen more and more often. Until—one day—in the end—

"Are you sure?" she asked.

"I am very sure, mademoiselle. But our offer remains a handsome one. Most of the character dancers are dancers who are no longer capable of anything else. We seldom provide a special training for character dancers. You might be wise to accept my proposal."

"Accept the Count's proposal!" echoed and enjoined Elena's Father from somewhere in the corner where the wastebasket stood. It was wonderful to see him still so agile.

"I should like time to think," said Elena, exactly as she had always been told to say, except by her Father and Mother.

"I have to go, mademoiselle, and I must tell you that the opportunity may not recur. It almost certainly will not."

Elena collapsed onto the divan which had been brought from Peshawar. "May I sit down?" she said.

But the Count remained standing, her Father pacing.

"You will not lose touch with home, Elena," said her Father. "Indeed, it will never be possible or acceptable for you to do that." He accompanied the professional phraseology by jingling the coins in his pocket, such as they were. He was near the tiger skin, now so faded that it might well have been the skin of a snow leopard or a yeti.

"It is right for me to tell you," said the Count, "that your training will be under the direction of Irash, who is the greatest character dancer in the world. Perhaps you have heard of him?"

"Irash!" exclaimed Elena's Father, who plainly had not.

Elena was very uncertain as to how far the Count's statement ought to settle the matter. But she found that she had sprung to her feet, defying all complexities. She had heard Irash's laugh, as if in the next room.

She nodded. She suspected that the Count had asked his question a little in irony, a usage to which she was still less habituated than Anna Ismailova.

"Life is far too short for uncertainty of any kind," admonished Count Oplotkin in his gentle voice, again smiling his gentle smile, and amiably bristling his gentle mustachio.

"Then I accept," said Elena. "Thank you."

"Thank God!" said Elena's Father, though less loudly than he usually said such things.

The Count gallantly shook Elena by the hand, bowing

gently over it. Elena could see how fond every single girl in the ballet must be of him.

"I shall send directions," he said. "Very soon. See to it that you keep up your full strength."

Only when the Count had gone did Elena's Father reveal that Count Wilmarazov-Totin, after being distraught for days, had suddenly destroyed himself, and that Rurik had been carried off, once and for all, though still without details vouchsafed, at least to Elena.

Farewells again! And now for longer! Or probably so!

O poor Silke! Never would Elena forget him altogether!

Never does anyone truly forget anyone or anything before the world has started its smudging!

There was a little more time on this occasion, and Tatiana's Mother offered a grand party with colored lights, snapdragon, ices, indoor fireworks, and a play in which everyone took part, entirely without preparation. Mademoiselle Olivier-Page had been asked to speak for all because she did it so purely and exquisitely, with never a word out of place. Clémence looked so proud of her elegant aunt that it was as if a nimbus shone round her small coiffure. Outside, the snow fell always.

Then it was for Elena to speak.

"I love you all," she said. "I shall love you till I die. Remember that I shall never be a ballerina. I shall be dancing only hags and goblins, and later perhaps the *Brockengespenst.*" It was a second German word she seemed to have picked up somewhere.

She held out both hands, and there was something in them.

"I give you this book," she said. "Remember me when you turn the pages."

Tatiana's Mother accepted Baron de la Touque's work on behalf of them all, in order that she might decide whether it was really suitable for everyone, especially as it had a bright green cover and a crimson silk marker and a wasp-colored band at the top edge.

All present clapped for a minute or two, and Ismene shouted out "We shall come and see you"; Clémence, usually the most fluent, being still enraptured.

No one had mentioned Anna Ismailova; not Tatiana, not Tatiana's Mother, not Elena.

In the end there was dancing: perfectly ordinary dancing, of course. Mikhail came in specially to play the balalaika, and brought his friend Tram, who possessed an accordion from Italy. Tatiana's Mother brought out a tambourine from Spain. A friend had been given it on her *lune de miel.* Now Tatiana rattled it about as if it had been she who was la Gitana.

The next morning Elena heard from Count Oplotkin's secretary about the coach that would come to collect her. She knew that it would be a very long journey, but she knew also that the railroad had been torn up for more than two versts by Nihilists, taking advantage of the weather.

She set out for the morning in no particular direction with Mikhail by her side. She was dressed in her own boots and furs, neither new nor *à la mode.*

Mikhail gazed around. "You would never have reached Smorevsk, Elena Andreievna, if Prince Popelevski had not found you."

"Of course I should, Mikhail Mikhailovitch. It was destined. A bear I met told me so." She was already falling into the way of such exaggerations. They everywhere are to be expected in and around a theater.

"We said we were destined for one another, Elena Andreievna."

"I expect we still are, Mikhail Mikhailovitch."

"For a second time, you are going away without me."

"I may come back."

"And then, the third time, we go together?"

"I am sure it will be like that, Mikhail Mikhailovitch. I am certain of it."

The freezing vapor that enclosed all things made playing upon a stringed instrument difficult, or even dangerous, so that once again Mikhail was without his balalaika. Even unaccompanied singing had its pulmonary perils, but Mikhail stood out for a stanza or two, unregarding.

> *Adieu is the bitterest word there is.*
> *Come back to me.*
> *The trees, the flowers, the stones, all weep.*
> *Come back to me.*
>
> *Adieu is a word of mystery to us all.*
> *Come back to me.*
> *Such answer as there is, lies in your heart.*
> *Come back to me.*
>
> *Adieu is the loveliest word there is,*
> *When thought is not given to what it means.*
> *I think, I feel, I suffer, and I fail.*
> *Come back to me.*

In the boundless snowy waste, the two of them were never once at a loss. Mikhail had to return a little early because his Mother was exalted, and there was no one else to help his Father in their tiny house.

The coach was calling very early the next day. The legs of dancers have far to go. Elena had told Mikhail, but no one else, as she had no wish to make things into a burden. Mikhail, therefore, was the only one to wave. He also doffed his worn fur hat as she passed in the snow, which she found a trifle chilling in more than the literal sense.

However, within the coach everything possible was present that might keep her warm. She waved back to Mikhail, no longer as a ballerina, but assuredly as what the Baron called a real woman. The red dress was in her Mother's reticule at her feet, even though it might seldom be needed.

She observed that only just outside the small town the air was full of double-headed eagles, difficult birds to number.